OCT 18

THE PIPER'S APPRENTICE

Also by Matthew Cody

The Secrets of the Pied Piper:
The Peddler's Road

The Secrets of the Pied Piper:
The Magician's Key

Powerless

Super

Villainous

The Dead Gentleman

Will in Scarlet

THE PIPER'S APPRENTICE

THE SECRETS OF THE PIED PIPER

BOOK III

Matthew Cody

ALFRED A. KNOPF
NEW YORK

For my brother Brian

THE PIPER'S APPRENTICE

❧ PROLOGUE ❧

A long time ago . . .

The fearless boy liked to wander the forests, even
though he'd been warned not to. He couldn't help
doing the things he'd been told not to do; it was just
in his nature to be contrary. He also couldn't help it if people insisted on calling him a young man, even though he still
felt very much like a boy on the inside. Adults always wanted
you to grow up too fast—mainly, the boy suspected, to in-
crease their numbers. The sooner you grew up, the sooner
you could be put to work, and that was your lot in life until
the grave.

So it would have been with the boy, if not for the Peddler. The boy owed the Peddler a kind thought, even if the
old magician (and so very, very old!) was a stick-in-the-mud,
always lecturing him about keeping to the road. The Peddler

had warned the boy to avoid all forests but the forest of the elves because there at least the Princess could look after him. But the boy didn't want looking after, and the Princess was no better than the Peddler with the way she lectured.

Therefore, when the Peddler was out roaming, the boy roamed as well, but he ventured into even darker places than he was warned about: Shades Harbor, to see the ghosts up close; the Shimmering Forest, to taunt nixies in their streams; the northern mountains, to trade baubles with goblins.

But the Bonewood was darkest of all. It was by far the most feared place on the Summer Isle, and certainly it was the most forbidden. Ogres roamed there, warned the Peddler, and worse things, too. It was the "worse things" now that intrigued the boy, since the ogres had turned out to be little threat. They were too big to sneak up on you, and the boy was far too clever to be caught.

So he strolled beneath the branches of bone, wrinkled his nose at the sickly sweet smell of grave moss. He hid in bushes and watched the ogres wrestle. If one caught scent of him, it was simple enough to play a charm to put the beast to sleep. A grim, dangerous place, to be sure, but also boring after a few days spent exploring. The boy began to wonder if the "worse things" even existed at all. Maybe they were as illusionary as the tales the cruel villagers back home used to frighten him with when he'd still been afraid—tales of men who turned into wolves by moonlight. That'd been one of the first things the boy had asked the Peddler when he'd arrived on this magic isle, wide-eyed and worried.

Do humans turn to beasts by moonlight here?

Poppycock! the Peddler had replied. *There're no humans here. You are the first.*

The boy had spent three sleepless nights terrified that *he* was going to turn into a wolf before the Peddler clarified what he meant. The Peddler might have looked like an ordinary old man, but he was something altogether different. The boy had heard differing rumors about the Peddler—the elves claimed he was the last of a race of mortal gods, while the kobolds said he was born of the very first potato left out in the sun when the world was new (most kobold origin stories had to do with root vegetables in one way or another).

To the boy, however, the Peddler was still the sour old magician who'd scooped him up out of poverty and hunger and given him a new life. But if the Peddler himself was to be believed, then the boy was the first and only truly human being to set foot on this isle of magic, and that made *him* special.

The boy had been called things before, horrible things, but he'd never been called special. It was the beginning of something new. In time he'd even come to believe it, and that belief washed away his fear and gave him the courage to follow his heart—a heart that often urged him to disobey.

But his heart grew tired of misbehaving for mischief's sake, and even exploring the Bonewood lost its thrill. One day, as his wanderings grew ever more listless and dull, he came across a small hut nestled in an especially dreary patch of forest. It had a lopsided roof hung with bone chimes that made an awful clatter when the wind picked up, like chattering ghouls playing a game of knucklebones beneath the Winter's Moon. Yet a curl of smoke drifted from the chimney, and the air was sweet with the smell of freshly baked pies.

The boy sneakily peeked in the window, because though he was fearless he was not stupid, and saw an old woman rocking in her chair by the fire. She looked human enough, if terribly old and ugly, but *looking* human and *being* human were two different things on the Summer Isle. Nixies looked human enough until they lured you into their ponds. Still, though caution was warranted, there was nothing here to be afraid of.

The boy knocked on the door.

He heard the creaking of the rocking chair and the old woman's groans as she hauled herself up to answer the door. When it opened, the boy saw that the woman was even uglier up close: hooked nose, warts and watery red eyes. And when she smiled, she revealed a mouthful of wooden teeth.

"A visitor?" she croaked. "And a boy, no less!"

She didn't call him a young man.

"I was passing by and saw your hut," said the boy. "I didn't think anyone lived in the Bonewood but ogres."

"And I didn't think children wandered this forest alone." An odd expression passed over the old woman's face, an unnerving eagerness he didn't care for. "But surely you smelled the pie baking. Wouldn't you like to come in and try a slice?"

The boy hesitated. "What kind?"

"Savory or sweet? You tell me."

"Well, I prefer sweet."

The old woman grinned. "And I usually likes 'em savory. . . . But you're in luck! It's cherry pie today."

The boy shrugged. Cherry pie sounded delicious, and he

supposed he could put up with the woman's ugly face for a slice of it.

She stepped aside. "There's a stool by the table there. Make yourself at home."

The boy stepped inside and took in the cluttered surroundings. Dried herbs hung from the ceiling. Jars and pestles littered the table, and besides the chair, bed and cooking pot, the only real piece of furniture was the massive oven. It was big enough to bake ten pies, at least.

Hanging from a peg behind the chair was a second set of fake teeth, only these were iron—and rusty. And jagged as a bear trap.

"Eh, I didn't catch your name, dear."

The boy hesitated again as he eyed the gruesome teeth hanging on the wall. "My mother warned me against giving away my name too freely. She said there were some who'd use it against me."

"Ah, don't you fret now about my good teeth," she said, noticing his wary stare. "Today's not a day for them. Today's a day for chatting and being hospitable." The woman hobbled back to her chair by the fire. "So what do you do, if you won't tell me who you are?"

The boy thought about it. The Peddler would call him an apprentice, though he could already do so much, he was tempted to tell her he was a full magician and be done with it. But the Peddler would be disappointed in him if he heard the boy was bragging. And as prickly as the old magician was, the boy still cared what the Peddler thought of him. When he wasn't breaking the Peddler's rules, he was trying desperately to impress him.

The boy decided instead on a simple answer, one both honest and true. "I'm a piper," he said, and he brandished a long, delicately carved flute.

The old woman clapped her hands together. "Oh, splendid! Could you play me a tune? Been a terrible long time since I heard proper music."

"I used to play for my supper."

"How about playing for a sweet dessert instead?"

So the boy brought the pipe to his lips and played a song of his own invention. Not quite a jig, but something light to bolster the spirits of an old woman living alone in the woods. A song easily worth a slice of pie.

As he played, the woman rocked in her chair and stamped her foot in time. A flash of movement, a scuttle across the floor, caught his eye—and when he turned around, an enormous rat was watching him, entranced.

He broke off his song with a yelp.

"Oh, he'll not hurt you. Not if you keep your distance."

With the end of the music, the rat seemed to remember itself, and its hackles raised as it hissed at the boy. It was at least as big as a cat, if not bigger.

"None of that, now," scolded the old woman. She reached into her pocket and pulled out a hunk of moldy cheese. "Here, take that and go back to your brothers." She wagged a bony finger in the rat's face as it scampered forward to claim its prize. "And no fighting! There's plenty to go around."

The rat snatched up the morsel and disappeared under the bed.

The boy began to worry about the cleanliness of the woman's hut. "That's the biggest rat I've ever seen."

"And getting bigger every day," said the woman. "Clever, too. Blame it on my home cooking."

"You know what, maybe I'll skip the pie after all."

"Hogwash! You played me a song and now you've earned your reward." She hauled herself out of her chair and to the oven. "Never seen them rats be that bold around strangers before. Think he liked your song, too."

The boy shrugged. "That happens sometimes. The Peddler says all music casts a spell, but mine is just stronger."

"The Peddler, you say? Well, he's a wise one."

"I guess. He used to teach me things. Doesn't so much anymore."

The woman made little noises as she used her apron to take the pie out of the oven. "Ooh, that's hot!" Then she took a wide-bladed knife from her belt and cut a slice. Trails of steam escaped as she served it up, and the soft center ran a dark crimson until it formed a slow-spreading puddle on the plate. She handed him a two-pronged fork and said, "Well, dig in!"

The pie was tart and delicious. "Where did you find the cherries? I didn't think much of anything grew in this forest except bonewood and grave moss."

"Got my secret ways."

"Aren't you going to eat?"

"Remember, I'm not wearing my good teeth this morning." The woman pointed to the iron teeth on the peg, then opened her mouth wide, showing the wooden ones fit snugly against her gray gums. "These'll do for now. We'll see how the day goes."

The boy finished his pie as the old woman watched him

eat, a satisfied grin on her face. He wondered again at the Peddler's warning against these woods. The ogres looked fierce, to be sure, but they were easy enough to avoid. Was this old woman the worst the Bonewood had to offer?

"Another slice?"

The boy wiped his face with his sleeve as he stood to go. "No, I'm stuffed."

"Well then, before you go on your way, would you do an old woman the favor of answering her a question?"

"I suppose."

"Why'd the Peddler stop teaching you?"

The boy felt his cheeks darken. He and the Peddler had quarreled the last time they'd spoken, and the boy had said some nasty things. Very nasty. He regretted them now. After all, the Peddler had rescued him from a beggar's life of hunger and woe. He'd brought the boy with him to this miraculous isle and taught him many secrets of magic. Just not all the secrets.

"The Peddler said I knew enough to take care of myself."

"And you agree?"

"No. I mean, yes, I can take care of myself, but no, it's not enough."

"If it's any use to you, I happen to agree." The old woman wiped her hands, which had become sticky with cherries, leaving red fingerprints on her apron. "This whole island is full of secrets. Enough to make a young magician powerful."

"I'm not a magician. I'm a piper."

"That's the Peddler talking."

"How do you know the Peddler, anyway?"

The woman sat down again in her rocking chair. "We've

known each other a long time. Since before we came to this isle. In the other place we knew each other. And there we fought. Oh, how we fought!"

A slight tingle of warning tickled the back of the boy's neck. The boy had never heard of anyone fighting the Peddler. Back home most people just ignored him, and in this place people respected him. The boy inched a step closer to the door. "Why did you fight?"

"Because of what I am," said the old woman. "Because some old dogs can't abide a thing acting according to its nature. Because I'm a witch."

A *witch.* The boy felt something tearing in his heart like a splinter. It conjured memories of furious men and women, the word spitting from their lips. Scared children hugging their mothers' skirts as their fathers hurled the word like a stone. Then they threw real stones.

It was always like this for the boy. Those memories were the only things that could make the fearless boy afraid. And that made him angry.

"That's what they called my mother," he said softly.

"A witch?"

The boy nodded. "The men and women of our village, just before they drove us out into the snow."

"What'd they call you? Not Piper, I'm sure."

"They called me the son of the witch."

The old woman stood again, only this time there was no stiffness in her bones. She stood tall and looked the boy in the eyes as she put her liver-spotted hand on his shoulder. "And you can call me Grannie. You and I are going to get along fine, my boy, my Piper. Just fine."

PART I

THE LONG WINTER

The ogre might not be able to see Carter, but that didn't mean it couldn't *smell* him. The great brute snuffled and sniffed its way through the underbrush below. From his hiding place in the branches of a tall pine tree, Carter could just make out the creature lumbering about as it scoured the trees for its missing meal. The ogre would stop, take a whiff or two at the base of the trunk, grumble in disappointment, and then move on to the next one. Sometimes it'd knock the disappointing tree over for good measure. Ogres were stupid—really stupid—but this one was at least bright enough to know that boys couldn't simply vanish. And what its beady eyes could not find, its enormous honker just might.

It was all the Pied Piper's fault.

If the Piper hadn't gotten a craving for dessert, and if he hadn't insisted that Carter conjure him up a cherry pie out of thin air, then Carter wouldn't have accidentally conjured said pie with such force that it exploded in his face.

Then Carter wouldn't have left the safety of their camp to find a stream to wash it all off. And he wouldn't have picked one that happened to be an ogre's favorite watering hole. That in itself was extremely odd—finding an ogre this far from the Bonewood. After escaping the elves, Carter and the Piper had emerged from the northeastern edge of the Deep Forest. For days now they'd been hugging the coast as they traveled south along the bluffs and crags of the Summer Isle's eastern shore. This ogre must've left his own forest and wandered until he reached the ocean. After shouting at it for a few days, he would have finally realized that the water wasn't about to move out of his way, and so he must've traveled south along roughly the same path as Carter and the Piper.

Lucky for Carter.

Ogres were big but slow, and this one carried a few extra folds of fat around his middle, so he hadn't been quick enough to catch Carter right away. He was, however, persistent enough to keep up the chase. He'd pursued Carter right into a copse of fir trees bordering a deep grotto. The trees were thick enough that the ground was mostly free of snow, so the ogre wouldn't be able to follow Carter's tracks. Carter had only needed to decide on climbing or going down. So he'd scrambled up the tallest tree he could find, one far taller than even the nine-foot-tall ogre, and hoped the beast would ignore the trees and search the grotto. Then Carter would quietly climb down and make his escape.

It would have worked, too. Because they towered over

most other creatures, ogres weren't in the habit of looking up, save during rainstorms. And then it was only to roar at the sky in confusion.

The ogre would've stomped right past Carter, unaware that the boy was hiding in the branches only a few feet overhead. It would have worked, if Carter hadn't still smelled like pie.

The Piper's fault. All of it.

But blaming someone else wouldn't keep Carter from becoming snack food. The ogre would find him eventually, by process of elimination if nothing else. There were only so many trees to knock down.

The only option now was magic. Carter would magic himself out of this mess. The problem was that since beginning his lessons with the Piper, Carter had been a spotty magician and still was—the cherry pie debacle proved that. The Piper claimed it was Carter's lack of focus that made his magic so unpredictable, and that, *by the way,* he'd have an easier time teaching a mayfly. It was true that Carter's magic did what he intended only about half the time. The other half, well . . . exploding pies.

The whole process of casting a spell hadn't turned out to be anything like Carter had imagined. There was no hand waving, no incantation in the Piper's magic. Recipes and rules were for hedge wizards and warlocks—strictly amateur stuff. Real magic was about finding your focus, like the Piper with his music. Once you had that, it was just about using magic to stack the odds in your favor. Magic was power and pure chaos. It was, by the Piper's definition, the unlikeliest of possibilities made to happen. Some places possessed more of it than others, though. But no matter the location, the basics were always the same—use your focus to bring order to chaos, and make it obey. Change the odds.

Carter had asked the Piper if it wasn't like the butterfly effect, whereby quantum physics stated that the flap of a butterfly's wings could set off a series of seemingly random events that led to a hurricane on the other side of the world. A hidden connectivity to the universe.

The Piper had blinked at him and said, "I prefer magic."

But Carter thought he saw a connection. For example, at that exact moment it would have been wonderful if the ogre down below simply took a nap. But what were the chances of that? Ogres didn't just fall asleep standing up, especially not when they were this close to a meal. The odds had to be a million to one. Or more.

That's where magic came in. Magic evened the odds, or better. The more unlikely a thing was, the harder the "spell" was to perform, but being a magician meant beating the odds. The really powerful magicians could do the impossible, like cause a cherry pie to appear out of nowhere.

With this in mind, Carter hoped that putting the ogre to sleep would be easier. Child's play compared to pie conjuring.

And yet Carter's palms were already sweaty despite the winter air, and his stomach roiled with nerves. He had no focus. The Piper had told him so again and again.

He could do this. He had to.

Despite the growling and the sniffing going on below him, Carter tried to relax, to breathe deeply like the Piper had taught him to. He closed his physical eyes and opened his mind's eye to "see" the magic all around him—auras, ley-lines. It was beautiful and unordered, an unrelated series of possibilities. Carter reached out and touched the magic, like plucking a guitar string, and the magic hummed in response. The air around him vibrated with it. He started a chain reaction.

He pictured the ogre. Pictured the beast's eyelids getting heavy. He conjured up a lullaby his mother used to sing to him when he was little:

Good night, my sweet.
Go to sleep.
In the morning,
I'll be here.

Carter opened his eyes and pointed at the ogre.
"Sleep," Carter commanded.
And he did. Carter fell fast asleep.

❈

He awoke with someone's hand clamped over his mouth. A shape leaned above him, a patchwork cloak pulled low over the person's face.

The Pied Piper held a finger up to his lips. "Shh," he whispered.

The fat ogre was lying on his back a few feet away, snoring contentedly. Carter nodded to the Piper that he understood the situation, one that was fairly easy to grasp—mustn't wake the ogre. Slowly, the Piper took his hand away. As Carter sat upright, he winced. He must've landed on his backside, because his butt felt like one enormous bruise. It was lucky, he guessed. He'd fallen ten feet at least out of that tree and slept through the impact. He could've broken his neck. But the spell was wearing off now, and if Carter was awake, then the ogre could wake any minute.

The Piper offered him a hand up, and for once Carter took it. Not far from where he'd landed, a squirrel lay curled up in a cozy ball, snoozing, too. And over there, a pair of robins slumbered, their heads tucked beneath their wings.

Carter had accidentally put himself to sleep with his own spell and, it appeared, every other creature in sight. It could have been worse. Carter looked at the snoring ogre, at the crooked teeth protruding from the beast's overly large mouth. Yes, it could have been much worse—Carter could've woken up in a cooking pot.

Did ogres bother with cooking pots? Probably not.

Gesturing for Carter to follow, the Piper padded noiselessly away. As Carter limped after him, he massaged his leg, to make sure nothing was hurt other than his bruised bottom. He adjusted his pack, feeling the shape of the plastic-and-metal leg brace tucked beside his rations and other supplies. There was a time not too long ago when Carter had limped everywhere, when he'd been trapped in that leg brace because of a foot that curled the wrong way. He still favored that leg and worried over his foot even though it had been magically healed.

The Piper sometimes teased him because he hadn't thrown the now-useless brace away, but he couldn't. Though he wouldn't admit it to the Piper, Carter lived in fear of the day that the spell might be broken. He lived in fear of being a cripple again.

Carter shook his head, trying to dislodge the ugly word from his brain. He'd been born with a bad leg, but he'd never been crippled. It wasn't Carter's word, and it never had been.

The Piper waited until they were safely back at their campsite before turning on Carter. "So, practicing on ogres now? Are you trying to get yourself killed?"

Carter met the Piper's angry stare. It was always unnerving because, though he was tall and lanky, the Piper looked barely more than a boy himself—fifteen perhaps. But those eyes of his were centuries old. Still, the days of the Piper being able to wither Carter with his ancient gaze were long past. The two had been through too much since then. Carter wasn't the Piper's prisoner anymore; he stayed with him out of choice. Which meant he didn't have to stand for the Piper's verbal abuse.

Carter took a deep breath. It wouldn't do to get into a shouting match, either. "I wasn't looking for an ogre. An ogre found me."

The Piper folded his arms across his chest. "And what was that bit of magic you used back there? Putting all those creatures to sleep with a single spell, including yourself! That's not something I've taught you."

"I wasn't . . . I was just trying to put the ogre to sleep so that I could get away." Carter pulled a clump of sticky pine needles out of his hair. "The rest were just collateral damage, I guess."

"You guess? Can you imagine what would've happened if the ogre had woken up first?"

Carter could imagine it. Quite vividly, and there was no cooking pot involved this time. "I didn't have any other choice, okay? It's not like another exploding pie would've done me any good."

"One minute you can't summon up a decent pie, and the next you practically put an entire forest to sleep with one spell." He studied Carter for a moment, his expression inscrutable. "What are the odds?"

"I failed again." Carter threw up his hands. "I was only aiming for the ogre. And I definitely wasn't trying to put myself to sleep."

"You need to focus—"

"I know."

"Dig deep, Carter. Where does your strength come from?"

"I eat my spinach."

The Piper stuck a long finger in Carter's face. "This is serious! You were nearly ogre food back there because you refuse to acknowledge the simple truth."

"Yeah? What's that?"

With a smirk, the Piper shrugged. "You're just like me. All our lives, it's been us against them. Me, because of who my mother was, and you, because of your lame foot. It's our anger at the world that focuses us!"

This again. Though Carter could barely follow his

twisted logic on most things, the Piper had made it very clear that he saw Carter as some kind of kindred spirit. And while it was true that Carter had struggled with his disability, he hadn't experienced anything close to the Piper's tragic childhood. Banished from his home, losing his mother—the Piper had a lot to be angry about.

But Carter wasn't the Piper.

With a frustrated sigh, he stomped over to the cold remains of their campfire and plopped down. He let out a yelp as his bruised butt hit the ground.

"Darn it!" Gingerly this time, he stretched out his legs and tried to scoot himself into a more comfortable position. It wasn't working, so eventually he gave up and rolled over on his side. "My butt's going to be black-and-blue in the morning."

"Healing is the most powerful of all." The Piper shook his head. "Witch's magic, or black magic as you like to call it, can't even touch it. But that doesn't mean healing's not dangerous, especially healing oneself. When a magician turns his magic upon himself, well, let's just say there's little room for error."

"I think I'll live with the bruised butt."

"Then again"—the Piper's eyes nearly twinkled with curiosity—"someone healed that leg of yours. Or *something?*"

Carter had been born with a clubfoot, and after several failed surgeries, he'd resigned himself to living his whole life with a brace around his leg. The Piper claimed that it was a sign that Carter was a child of prophecy—the last son of Hamelin and a descendant of Timm Weaver, a child who himself had suffered a lame foot. Timm was also the only child of Hamelin left behind by the Piper. Regardless, his disability was something Carter had learned to accept. But then he'd come to the Summer Isle and, after some time, his leg had miraculously healed.

"Okay," said Carter. "So are you saying that neither one of us healed my leg? That it just healed itself?"

The Piper shrugged. "No, but I wonder if a single child has gotten sick after coming to this isle. Has there been one cold? So much as a sniffle? I'm over seven centuries old by your measure, and yet I look like a young man in my teens." He leaned in close and winked. "I wouldn't put it past the isle to have fixed that leg of yours, too. Not such a bad place after all, eh? And they call me a villain for bringing the children of Hamelin here!"

"We've been over this. The word you're looking for is *kidnapping*—you kidnapped those children just like you kidnapped me and my sister."

"Bah." The Piper threw his hands up. "You sound like a mockingbird. The same thing over and over and over . . ."

But Carter was just getting started. "Look around this place. It's winter in the Summer Isle, and the days have gotten so short, I'm afraid they'll disappear altogether. And you still insist this is some kind of paradise!"

"Oh? And you're so keen to leave, are you? You want to go back to a world where people get old, get sick and even die! What do you think'll happen to that leg of yours then, eh? Here's a rule of magic for your lessons—what's been done with magic can be *undone*."

And just like that they were in one of their standoffs again. These arguments flared up daily, and it seemed like anything could set one of them off. Normally the two would retreat to corners and stew for a few hours while they let their tempers cool.

But today was different. Carter looked down at his leg—his perfectly healthy leg. What *would* happen when . . . if . . . he ever got back home?

Like it or not, the Piper was the only source of information Carter had. So he swallowed his anger and took a deep breath. "Piper, I have a question."

But the Piper remained silent, his back turned. He stayed huddled in his pied cloak near the fire.

Carter rolled his eyes. For a centuries-old magician, the Piper really did act like a spoiled kid sometimes. "Excuse me, *Teacher*?"

The Piper glanced over his shoulder. "You know, I called my teacher *Master*."

"Oh, come on!"

"Fine, fine." The Piper held up his hands. "It irked me to do it, too. What do you want to know?"

"Back in the real world—I mean *our* world—does magic still exist?"

"Hmm. I imagine it does, but it's hard to find there. Less obvious. It would take quite the magician to make it work. When you look for the magic, what do you see?"

Carter thought about this. When he closed his eyes, he could feel the magic around him. More, he could actually *see* it in his mind. "It's like lines of power all around. Almost like threads tying everything together."

The Piper nodded. "Then think of the Summer Isle, well, as the center of an unfinished tapestry, and all those threads are loosely woven. All possibilities intertwine, and here anything is possible. Back home, reality is settled. The pattern's finished and the knots are harder to untie."

"So earth legends and stories about famous magicians, like Merlin and stuff—those could've been real people?"

"Yes. But remember this, Carter—human beings like us were not *meant* to meddle with magic. Witches and elves were born with magic in their blood; it's a part of them. But for us, it's a dangerous business. That's why when the Peddler taught me, he insisted I go slowly. He only showed me the most basic tricks. Boring stuff, really."

"You mean like conjuring pies?"

The Piper ignored Carter's comment and continued. "He said he was afraid I'd hurt myself if I tried too much too fast, but I thought he was worried I'd turn out to be a better magician than he was."

The Piper sat across from Carter and reached into his cloak. From some hidden pocket, he produced a delicate wooden flute. He played a simple tune, his fingers gliding up and down the instrument with skill. In response to the Piper's song, the campfire roared to life.

"The truth is," said the Piper, "he was right. Even small magic can be deadly if you can't control it. Like a simple campfire can grow to consume a forest, so it is with magic."

Carter thought about how he'd lost control of his sleep spell. What if he'd been trying something more destructive against the ogre—what might have happened then?

He tried to shake away the troubling thought and scooted closer to the fire. This winter showed no signs of weakening, and in fact the days were only getting shorter. There was a time, not too long ago, when the Summer Isle had lived up to its name, but those days were over. He stretched his chilled fingers closer to the flames and tried to rub life back into them.

"You have a new pipe?"

The Piper nodded. "I finished carving it while you were out on your adventure."

Carter rolled his eyes at the word *adventure*—"main course" was more like it—but he didn't bother arguing the point.

"So if the ogre had woken up, you could've handled it. With magic."

The Piper shrugged. "Probably. But these toys"—he held up the little flute—"break too easily." He leaned forward, his expression hungry. "I need my pipe back, Carter. The one I learned on. It's mine."

And they were back to this. The real reason they were together. It wasn't to teach Carter to be a magician. The Piper stayed with Carter because he wanted Carter's help finding his lost pipe, the enchanted flute he'd used all those hundreds of years ago to steal away the children of Hamelin. Oh, there were other purposes, the Piper claimed. He warned that a war was coming, and he hinted that he and Grannie Yaga would be on opposite sides, although Carter found that hard to believe. Grannie had delivered Carter to the Black Tower, where the Piper had used Carter to escape his prison. Now the Piper claimed he and Grannie Yaga were no longer allies.

Possibly. But just as likely the two were manipulating Carter again so that the Piper could return to his full strength.

"Magic may seem to you like a great weaving of threads," the Piper was saying. "But to me it's music. Every magician perceives its mystery in a different way. My magic is made up of notes most people can't hear. I shape it into song, and that's where my power comes from. But you've seen what happens to these shoddy instruments when I try to reach for too much."

Carter had. The Piper's jail cell floor had been littered with the splintered remains of shattered flutes. Carter still wasn't sure how it worked exactly, but there was something special about the Piper's original pipe, or something special about his relationship to it. He wanted it back more than anything in the world.

And Carter would stop him from getting it. The closer he stayed, the better he could keep an eye on the Piper. At least that's what he told himself. It was what he repeated when the little voice inside him suggested he was staying with the Piper, the villain who'd kidnapped him in the first place, because he was learning magic. Even if his magic was still only so-so.

"If you want your pipe back so badly," said Carter, propping himself up on one elbow, "then why don't you go get it yourself? You've already admitted you know where it is."

"I know that the Peddler hid it at Magician's Landing, but do you think that old wizard just tossed it into a box?" The Piper stared into the fire, and the dancing flames reflected in his eyes. "Finding where it was hidden was the easy part."

"And you think I can help?"

The Piper's gaze flicked from the fire to Carter. The flames still danced in his eyes. "You freed me from the Black Tower by simply being there. Your touch unlocked a prison the most powerful magic in the Summer Isle couldn't open." He paused. "Yes, I think you can help."

That was precisely what Carter had feared. The Piper wanted to come and go from the Summer Isle as he pleased. He'd stolen away the children of Hamelin. Recently he'd kidnapped Carter and his sister, and once threatened to steal even more children away, to bring them here to this hidden land of magic, where they could stay young forever. The Piper really had convinced himself he was doing them a favor. He was that delusional and that dangerous.

Carter had to stop him before that happened. And every little piece of magic he learned gave him a better chance to do so.

He hoped.

"In any case," said the Piper, interrupting Carter's train of thought, "we have much to do between here and there. There's still so much to teach you." Then he pulled his hood down low over his face and lay back with his arms clasped behind his head. "Beginning with how to summon a pie that doesn't explode. Maybe an apple walnut this time?"

⟨ CHAPTER TWO ⟩

The bridge was supposed to be there. It used to be there. Where the Shimmering Forest ended and the Western Fork of the Great River split the Summer Isle nearly in two, an enormous stone bridge spanned the river. Except now it didn't.

Max and Lukas had set out from New Hamelin one week ago to find Max's lost brother. They followed the same route as before—the one they'd traveled with Carter, Emilie and Paul back when this whole adventure began. They marched south along the Peddler's Road past the Shimmering Forest, but this time the road was rocky and overgrown with treacherous thorns, and the days were short and the nights dark and brutally cold. Instead of a summer breeze at their backs, they were met with a fierce winter headwind that slowed their every step. By the time they reached the river, they were days behind where they wanted to be.

And now, the bridge was missing.

"How can a bridge just disappear?" asked Max.

"Easy," replied Lukas. "It walks away."

Particularly if the bridge in question was a troll bridge. Not a bridge where a troll made his home, but a real troll who'd turned to stone either by age or by sunlight as he was wading across the river.

The last time they had traveled the Peddler's Road, the troll bridge had been right there, a weathered span of lumpy stone vaguely troll-shaped. Now all that remained were a few boulders along the shore and a trail of massive craters in the muddy bank—footprints—leading south.

"Look here," called Lukas. The Eldest Boy of New Hamelin, Captain of the Watch, was examining one of the half-buried boulders in the muck. "You know what? I think the old fellow went off and forgot a few of his toes. See?"

He was pointing to one edge of the boulder where, beneath the blanket of lichen and moss, something like a jagged stone toenail could be seen poking out.

"Eww," said Max.

But Lukas only shrugged. "Don't think he misses them. He's mostly a pile of rocks anyhow."

"Well, I wish he'd waited until we'd made it safely across the river before deciding to take a stroll. How long did you say he'd been in there?"

"As long as I can remember," said Lukas.

Centuries, then. Max didn't say it out loud, but she was thinking it. Winter. The sun setting every night. Now this. Change had come to the Summer Isle, and it had come suddenly.

"It's this weather." Lukas held out his hand and let a snowflake melt on his open palm. Flurries had been drifting from the clouds all morning long, but thankfully nothing more than that. Storms came swiftly and unexpectedly these days. "It's not going to make the road any easier."

✻

"We'd better get a move on before something worse than a walking bridge shows up." Max hauled a coil of rope over her shoulder. "Break time's done. Help me tie the rest of these logs."

Max had never built a raft before. Another one to add to her list of bizarre firsts since coming to the Summer Isle. She'd opened magical portals, speared giant rats. She'd even led an army into battle. Raft-building was tame by comparison.

Lukas bent down and examined their handiwork. It'd taken the entire day to collect enough driftwood to cobble together a raft barely wide enough to carry both of them. They'd already used most of the rope they'd brought from New Hamelin, and after they'd finished tying the last of the logs, that would be gone.

Lukas gave the raft a shake. "Still a lot of gaps here and here." He pointed to the section Max had just tied off.

"It's not like we're taking it out on a river cruise," snapped Max. It annoyed her that her contributions were always the ones Lukas nitpicked over. "The raft only needs to make it from one side of the river to the other."

"Do you really want to risk it? If we get wet, it's going

to be very hard to get dry again. We could freeze to death before we find your brother."

Carter. Max didn't need to be reminded of their real purpose for being out there, but Lukas always brought him up anyway. Her brother was somewhere beyond the river. Hopefully, he and Leetha were safe among the elves in the Deep Forest, as had been the plan. Hopefully, he was warm and dry.

But hope had a way of betraying you in the Summer Isle, and both Lukas and Max worried about him. Leetha was a daughter of the elves, and a fighter who was used to taking care of herself. But there was a feeling neither Max nor Lukas could shake, that Carter was in terrible danger.

Max knew that Lukas felt responsible for Carter, since he'd allowed her brother to set out on his own with Leetha while Lukas and the others headed back to New Hamelin. But Max didn't blame him. He'd thought he was doing the right thing by sending Carter to stay with the elves. And she knew that Lukas, boy Captain of the Watch, was still reeling from the revelation that his friends, once thought lost, were still alive.

Alive, but held as slaves by the rats. Marc, Leon and so many other children of New Hamelin who'd been captured in rat raids over the many years, or who'd simply gone missing, were being forced to serve the rat king.

And still, Lukas was here helping her. Max was grateful, even if she was having a hard time showing it.

An ice floe drifted downriver. Not enough to block their way across, not yet, but still thick enough to make it treacherous. Lukas was right: if they tried to make the river crossing on a leaky raft, they'd end up with frostbite or worse.

Lukas drew his sword, the black iron Sword of the Eldest Boy.

"Whoa!" Max held up her hands. "Okay, we'll fix the raft. No need for violence."

He ignored her joke. Like two siblings on a long road trip, they'd stopped making each other laugh days ago. "I'll dig up some clay from the riverbank, and we can use that to fill in the holes. The ground's frozen, so it might take me a while."

While Lukas dug for clay, Max did an inventory of their supplies for what must've been the hundredth time. The rope was mostly gone, but they had packs of rations enough to last several weeks if they were smart with them. Flint and tinder for campfires, spare cloaks treated with pig fat to keep the worst of the moisture off. Max's spear and Lukas's sword for protection.

And in Max's backpack, the most precious parcel of all—two glass jars wrapped carefully in soft cloth. These Max kept a close eye on day and night.

After the Pied Piper had magically lured Max and her brother to the Summer Isle, Grannie Yaga had snatched up Carter and delivered him to the Piper's prison in the Black Tower. Long ago, the witch had spoken a prophecy that the last son of Hamelin, whom she believed to be Carter, would release the Piper and eventually lead the children of Hamelin home again. In an attempt to free Carter, Max had fallen through a magic portal that took her back home to the real world. But in her quest to return to the Summer Isle to res-

cue her brother, she learned that the creatures of magic—
elves, kobolds, witches—had given up the real world for the
Summer Isle long centuries past. And as with any exodus,
there were those who'd been left behind. Their descendants
had lived for the most part in hiding, until a wicked magician named Vodnik appeared. He promised he could unlock the last door to the Summer Isle, for a price.

But Vodnik had lied. Instead, he took everything they
had and left them stranded in the tunnels beneath New
York City, in a dismal place called Bordertown. When Vodnik learned that Max had actually traveled to the Summer
Isle and back again, he tried to blackmail her into showing
him how to unlock the door for real.

For leverage, he trapped the souls of her parents in two
glass jars.

Vodnik was dead now, and Max had led the Bordertowners through the magic door to the Summer Isle herself, but the magician's curse on her parents lived on. Until
Max could find another magician powerful enough to safely
break the spell, she would keep those two jars safe with
her life.

Find Carter.

Break Vodnik's curse and set their parents free.

Go home.

"We've already lost two days. What's a few more hours?"
Max let her question hang in the air. Days. How many days
had she been on the Summer Isle this time? How many
since she'd left Hamelin, and her old life, behind? Time was
fuzzy here, and the longer you stayed, the fuzzier it got, but
she tried some quick estimates in her head.

"Hey, Lukas, you know what?" Max stood and wiped her filthy hands on her already filthy jeans. "I think it's my birthday! Or yesterday was. Maybe the day before. I can't tell for sure in this place, but I'm pretty sure I just turned thirteen!"

Lukas gave her a look. "How's it feel?"

"Like twelve. Darn it."

"I'm not surprised." Then he shrugged and walked away.

That was it. No fuss, not even a "should have baked you a cake" joke. Just that. Max had been expecting at least some congratulations. . . .

Then it hit her. Lukas probably didn't even remember his own birthday. He might've looked like a boy her age, but like the rest of the New Hameliners, he'd been trapped here on the Summer Isle for ages. How long ago had he stopped bothering to keep track? Time on the Summer Isle blurred and stretched in ways that made it seem more like dream time than real time. It would be hard to count the days, much less the centuries. Even if you wanted to.

And here she was bragging about turning thirteen. What did she want, a party and presents? Max and Lukas were on a mission to find her brother. Until that happened, birthdays were meaningless. They had more pressing things to worry about, like getting across the darn river.

So Max used the last of their rope to reinforce the raft's bindings, shaking them, testing the logs in places she'd seen Lukas do.

"You'd better float," she whispered to the raft. "You'd just better."

Float it did. Though it bobbed precariously as they pushed off from shore, the little clay-and-driftwood craft supported their weight well enough. Water seeped through cracks they couldn't see, but not enough to sink the raft.

They used Max's spear to break up the ice near the shore, and then to pole themselves out until the water was too deep to touch bottom. Then Lukas paddled with a makeshift oar fashioned from a split log, while Max continued to use the spear to clear a path through the ice. Staying completely dry on their leaky little raft was impossible, and Max looked forward to sitting in front of a cozy fire on the far shore. As long as they weren't completely soaked, they should be able to dry off before nightfall.

By the time they reached the river's deeps, Max's shoulder muscles burned from exhaustion, even as the icy water froze her toes numb. And they were still only halfway there. The current had pulled them farther downriver than they'd planned, and the road ahead was little more than a distant squiggle in the snow. Soon it'd be out of sight entirely.

They were going to lose even more daylight trying to find the road again. If they drifted much farther south, they'd have to wait until morning to search for it—it was too dangerous roaming around in the dark, with wet clothes no less. All because the Summer Isle didn't know what a proper bridge was, one that didn't get up and wander off.

The current grew sluggish as the ice floe thickened. Max

was fumbling to move a stubborn patch of ice out of their way when a shadow passed overhead, like a cloud drifting in front of the sun. But the sun was already hidden behind the constant overcast sky. What could make the day even darker than it already was?

"Max! Get down!"

Lukas moved to grab her, but Max had already thrown herself flat on the raft as he'd commanded. Something heavy flew above them. She rolled to one side and looked up in time to see an ugly fat goose squawking at them as it made for shore. It had missed Max by mere inches.

When the goose reached the riverbank it transformed. Feathers became a patched skirt and a handkerchief. Beak became a hooked nose and a pointed, warty chin.

The witch of the Bonewood, Grannie Yaga, stood on the river's far shore and peered at them through her one good eye. The other had been taken out by Paul's arrow in the siege of New Hamelin. Right before she stopped the boy's heart with a curse.

Lukas, who'd ducked down next to Max, pulled himself to one knee and drew his sword.

"Tut, tut, boy," called Grannie. "Still an awful lot of river between us, and you won't be getting close enough to use that poker on me this time."

She held up a gnarled hand and her sleeve fell away to reveal a wicked-looking burn along her forearm. Lukas had given her that with one touch of the sword when she'd threatened Emilie. The iron of the Eldest Boy held some magic that acted as proof against her witchery.

Max gripped her spear. Could she hit the witch with it

from there? She doubted it. She'd proven herself a decent enough fighter with the weapon, but mostly in the stick-you-with-the-pointy-end style of fighting. She didn't have a particularly strong throwing arm.

But she was tempted to try.

"I come to talk to the girl there." Grannie was still wearing her horrible iron teeth. Rust and blood stained the corners of her mouth where the sharp points bit into her lips.

"Why would I want to talk to a murderer?" spat Max.

"You mean what I done to the Peddler? That was war, sweetie. And I won."

"Not just the Peddler. My friends told me what you did to Paul."

Grannie made a *tsk*ing sound. "Ah, the poor boy. The little archer. Well, lookit here what he done to old Grannie first." She angled her face so that Max could get a good look at the empty eye socket. It was a puckered and angry red wound. "What he got was payback. Fair's fair."

During the siege of New Hamelin, when Lukas's walled village was being attacked by rats and ogres, Grannie had appeared with an offer. She'd promised to call off the attackers if they gave Carter up, but Grannie hadn't known that Carter was miles and miles away on the other side of the isle. Enraged, Grannie had threatened the lives of the youngest New Hameliners, and Lukas, Emilie and Paul had fought the witch to a standstill.

In the end, Max had arrived with her own army to break the siege, but not in time to save Paul from Grannie's death magic. At least the brave young scout had left his mark on the witch.

"What do you want from us?" asked Max.

Lukas shot her a warning glare, but she ignored it.

"There's a sensible girl." Grannie wiped a trickle of dark spittle from her chin. Those teeth of hers weren't made for talking. "Your brother was my guest not so long ago. Polite boy. Well-mannered. I liked him."

Carter had been Grannie's prisoner, not her guest, but Max decided not to argue the point. "You came to New Hamelin looking for him. Why?"

"I lent him to the Piper, so's the Piper could get free of that nasty cell. But a loan is not a gift. I want the boy back."

"He's my brother," said Max. "He doesn't belong to you."

Lukas, Max noticed, was slowly edging himself in front of her. "Stay behind me," he whispered.

"I'm not—"

"Just do it!"

"Huh?" Grannie cupped a liver-spotted hand against her ear. "What's that you two darlings are going on about? Rude to whisper in front of your elders."

Max tried to get out from behind Lukas—she could take care of herself.

"We were saying that you'll never get Carter, you old hag!" said Max.

"Ah, but I'm not just asking," said Grannie. "Tell me where the boy is, or you'll both suffer for it."

Max tried to aim her spear at the witch, but Lukas was still in the way. "Stay behind me!" he whispered.

What was Lukas doing? At that moment Max wasn't sure who she was angrier with, the witch or Lukas.

Grannie Yaga cackled. "Maybe a little hurting would loosen those tongues?"

The witch lifted her hand and with a flick of her wrist conjured what looked like black tendrils of smoke. They slithered across the water, just above the surface like morning fog. When they reached the raft, the tendrils reared up, like snakes preparing to strike. Max and Lukas bravely held their weapons at the ready. Then as the creatures attacked . . . they disappeared. They literally went up in smoke.

"What happened?" asked Max. But then she saw: Lukas had the Sword of the Eldest Boy in his hands. He was holding it up in front of them, barring the snakes' attack. Max could feel warmth emanating from the blade.

She understood. Lukas had told her that the sword had protected him from Grannie Yaga's killing curse back at the siege, that her magic hadn't been able to affect him. But he'd been too far away from Paul to save him, too. Lukas wasn't being chauvinistic by standing in front; he was trying to protect them both from Grannie's sorcery.

Max inched herself closer to the boy.

Grannie also realized what was happening, however, and she let out an awful snarl. "Curse that blade! That old Peddler is six feet under dirt and his magic is still a needle in my eye."

"You can't hurt us!" shouted Lukas. "And you'll never find Carter!"

"Won't I? I'm guessing that the boy's not in New Hamelin anymore, or else the sister wouldn't have left the village. And since you two were traveling east, then maybe that's where Grannie should start hunting. Did you hide him in the Deep Forest? You think that'll keep him safe from me?" The witch stepped to the river's edge. "That sword of yours may protect you from Grannie's magic, but it don't protect the whole river."

"What's she mean?" whispered Max. "She can't hurt the river!"

Grannie lifted her hand to her mouth and bit into the meaty flesh of her palm. Then she held her hand out over the water, and blood the color of black cherries seeped out of the wound and began to drip. As soon as the witch's blood made contact with the water, the river began to churn. What was one moment a slowly flowing current became as rough as a storm-tossed sea. The ice floe that had been blocking them cracked and splintered. Max and Lukas had to drop to their hands and knees to hang on as their raft was nearly upended.

The raft began to buckle as the current spun it in circles, pulling it farther downriver as Grannie Yaga's laughter rang in the distance.

CHAPTER THREE

The raft held together at first. Despite the churning waves Grannie Yaga had conjured with her witch's blood, both Max and Lukas managed to hold on to the raft for as long as it stayed afloat. But they were amateur shipwrights at best, and as Max had said, their little craft was only meant to carry them from one bank to the other. It hadn't been built to withstand these conditions.

Ice water spilled over the sides. The angry river spun them in circles and slammed the raft into the ice floe again and again. Max was slipping, and her frozen fingers could barely find purchase. Lukas rolled dangerously near the edge.

The raft still rocked, but gently now, in rhythm to an unsung lullaby. Max opened her eyes and blinked up at the bright sun directly overhead. A small break in the bleak clouds had opened, and Max lifted her head just to feel the warmth on her face. It didn't last long, a minute or two, but while it did she drank it in.

The next thing she did was search her backpack to make sure her parents' jars were still there and intact. She breathed a sigh of relief, then took stock of her surroundings. They were on the raft, though she must've blacked out some time ago. Lukas was lying at her side, his arms wrapped around her. The boy's lips were pale from the cold, but he was breathing easily. They'd held on to each other for support as the raft tumbled around them, and that had been enough to make sure neither one of them got tossed overboard. The raft itself was missing a few planks, but it was still afloat. Thank goodness Lukas had insisted on filling in every little leak.

She plucked a string of river weed from his matted hair. "I hate to say it, so I'll say it while you're still asleep: you were right about the raft."

"I know," he mumbled, and slowly opened his eyes.

Max flung the river weed back at him. "How long have you been awake? Just lying there, pretending to be asleep?"

"No." Lukas lifted himself to one elbow. "I've been lying there wondering if I was going to be sick."

He barely made it to the side of the raft before puking. After he was finished, he rolled onto his back. "Well, there's our answer," he said weakly.

Seeing it happen, hearing it happen, made Max's own stomach queasy. Not so long ago she'd made an ocean voyage and spent most of it hovering over a bucket. She did not want to repeat the experience.

"Where are we?" She stood up on unsteady legs and looked around. "We need to get off this raft."

The trees of the Shimmering Forest were gone, and the sloping riverbanks had been replaced by steep cliff faces of rock on either side. Well ahead of them, the river widened and spilled out into a fog-shrouded bay. Seagulls cawed to each other in the distance.

Lukas sat up, with some difficulty, and said, "I think we drifted downriver all the way to the sea."

"Well, let's hope not!" Max looked around for one of their makeshift paddles, but of course they were long gone. Lukas had managed to keep his sword scabbarded at his side, but her weapon was gone. "Man, every spear I get ends up at the bottom of a river."

Even if the water was shallow, without her spear they wouldn't be able to pole themselves to shore. Not that the shore was very inviting. The sheer cliff faces rose at least thirty feet on each side, and other than a few sandbars there weren't any places to ground their raft.

"Guess we follow the current," said Lukas.

"What? And just drift out to sea?"

Lukas shook his head. "We won't make it that far."

"And why not?"

"Because the river will take us out past those cliffs, but after that . . ."

"What?"

"Look at that mist," said Lukas. "Does it look a little familiar?"

Max squinted. It was still a ways off, and mostly obscured by the cliffs, but she could see up ahead a frozen bay. Fog hung in a low cloud over everything, broken only by steeple roofs along the shore and the masts of icebound ships.

"Shades Harbor," said Lukas. "We're headed for the village of ghosts."

❖

Winter had come to Shades Harbor as well but hadn't improved it. The port village was always a gray place, shrouded as it was in perpetual mist, but now the mist carried a winter chill. The buildings were a mismatch of sizes and shapes, but the style was fairly consistent—what Carter would call "sad-chic." Roofs sagged with snow as well as age, and icicles dangled from lonely shop signs. The peeling paint and empty windows would lead one to think that the village was abandoned, but Max knew that wasn't the case at all. There were plenty of residents; you just couldn't always see them.

Shades Harbor was haunted by restless spirits. Mostly they were shades who came on great black ships, souls on their way to the afterlife. These souls lingered in Shades Harbor for a time, until they gradually accepted the truth of their fates—that they really were dead. Then their invisible spirits would board the black ships once more to whatever final destination awaited them. Only those black ships were now frozen in place, stuck in the thick ice that was once the bay.

Though the ice near the village wharf was too thick to sail into, the children were able to dock their ramshackle raft along the rocky beach that ringed the bay in a rough semicircle. From there they approached the village on foot. As unwelcoming as Shades Harbor was, at least it was dry land. If they didn't dawdle there, they wouldn't be in much danger.

"If we follow the pass north out of town, it will meet up with the Peddler's Road," said Lukas as they clambered over rocks slick with frost. "What's left of it, anyway. But we have to be more careful now. Grannie Yaga failed to drown us, but we're way off our path. We're farther south than I would've liked, and that means we'll have to pass the Bonewood. Again."

Max grimaced. "Grannie's home turf."

"It might not matter. These days Grannie could attack from anywhere, as we've seen. I don't think there's anyplace in the Summer Isle safe from her now, except maybe the elves' forest."

"It'd better be." Not only was Max counting on finding her brother safe and sound with the elves, she was also hoping that the Princess would be able to free their parents' souls.

"I'm worried about the other dangers in the Bonewood." Lukas adjusted his sword in its scabbard. "Ogres, mainly. We need to be on the lookout."

Max threw up her hands. "Can we please make it through the haunted village in one piece before you start in with all the other terrible things in our way? One at a time, please."

Even though Max had meant it as a tease, a little bit of dark humor to lighten the mood, the boy blushed and looked away. "You're right," he said. "I apologize."

It was easy to forget how much Lukas blamed himself

for the mess they were all in. It had been Lukas who'd convinced them to set out on the Peddler's Road in the first place. After the Pied Piper had stolen Max and Carter away to the Summer Isle, Lukas and the rest of the lost children of Hamelin took them in and protected them, but it hadn't been for purely selfless reasons. Lukas had been betting that Carter was the son of Hamelin mentioned in the prophecy: *Only when the last son of Hamelin appears and the Black Tower found will the Piper's prison open and the children return safe and sound.* Despite the ominous warning about the Piper's prison, Lukas had worked hard to convince Max and Carter that finding the Black Tower would show them all the way home again.

He'd been wrong. Instead, they'd gotten the Peddler killed, freed the Piper from centuries of imprisonment and allowed evil to reign over the land. At least that's how Lukas saw it.

Max saw things differently. None of this was their fault. It was all because of the Pied Piper of Hamelin. He'd originally been imprisoned for kidnapping the children of Hamelin, locked in the Black Tower by the combined powers of the Peddler and the Princess. It was only later, after Grannie Yaga had spoken her prophecy, that he'd begun his plan to kidnap Carter as well. From within his cell he used a magic mirror to reach across worlds to modern-day Hamelin, and pluck Carter (and, perhaps accidentally, Max) from their own kitchen. With Grannie's help, Carter was brought before the Piper and used against his will to break the magical lock that had kept the Piper prisoner all those years. Max was tossed back into the real world and had to battle a soul-stealing magician to return to the Summer Isle, but she did it.

The Peddler was dead now at the hands of the witch Yaga, and the Princess hadn't emerged from her castle in the Deep Forest for centuries.

Paul was dead. Emilie, Eldest Girl of New Hamelin; Harold the loyal trollson; even their old elfling housekeeper, Mrs. Amsel, were all helping to rebuild the village in case of another attack. It was up to Max and Lukas to find Carter on their own. No one was left to help them.

Thanks to the Piper.

As the pair wandered along the waterfront, they kept a wary eye on the shadows between buildings, on the alleyways. Although it was said ghosts didn't usually bother the living, Paul had warned them of rumors that gray men lived in the dark places of this village. The gray men were supposed to be legends only, but Max had seen one conjured in the Piper's cell. They were said to be the souls of murderers who'd refused to move on to the afterlife, spirits who hated the living and shunned the sun. And there was little daylight left.

The village square looked empty, but sounds drifted by on the wind. Spectral voices belonging to people who weren't there. Soon they were loud enough that if Max closed her eyes, she could imagine the square busy with people—fishermen, merchants, even children at play. Every now and again she felt someone bump into her. A child muttered an apology as she brushed past.

But when Max opened her eyes again, there was only Lukas and the lonely, empty streets.

"Let's get out of here," said Max quickly. "I don't want to spend another minute in this place."

Lukas nodded. The boy was worried about camping in the wilderness so near the Bonewood, but he felt the wrongness of this village, too. The unseen residents of Shades Harbor were agitated, restless. It was a marked change from the last time Max and Lukas had visited, when they'd gone almost unnoticed.

Hurrying, they headed for the main street out of town, where the cobblestones would give way to the dirt path that led north to the Peddler's Road. As they passed by the old inn where they'd stayed last time, Max stopped.

"Lukas," she said. "Look."

A room on the top floor was lit. A single candle burned in the window.

"That's the room we stayed in, isn't it?" said Lukas. "Yes, it is. Corner room, third floor. That's where we stayed when we were here with . . ."

Lukas's sentence trailed off as he was struck by the very same thought that Max was having. That's where they'd stayed with Carter.

"Wait, Max," he said. "We can't rush in."

But Max had already pushed past the boy. If for some reason Carter hadn't made it to the elves' forest, then he would've followed the road to New Hamelin. It was possible that he'd decided to stop off here, especially if he thought it was a safer bet than spending the night outdoors.

Max barged into the inn. Empty shelves and empty tables. Cobwebs and frost. But there in the thick dust were fresh footprints. Max took the stairs to the second floor, two at a time. Lukas followed, pleading with her to slow down.

More footprints on the top floor, crisscrossing the hallway outside the door to their old room.

The only thing that had kept Max from going insane with worry for these past few days was the belief that her brother was safe with the elves. But what if he wasn't? What if he'd been traveling through this bleak winter all alone, trying to find his way back to his friends?

"Carter!" Max cried as she threw open the door.

Inside, a cloaked figure stood next to the window, face hidden beneath a hood.

Max's heart sank. Whoever this person was, he was Max's height at least—too tall to be her brother. Lukas squeezed through the doorway, his sword drawn and held cautiously in front of him.

"Who's this?" he whispered.

"I don't know," answered Max, crestfallen. "But it's not who I was hoping for."

"If it's any consolation," said the cloaked figure, pulling down the hood, "you're not who I was hoping for, either."

Blond hair in a tight bun. A pair of blue eyes that Max knew well. She'd been on the receiving end of that disapproving stare enough times to never forget it.

"Emilie?" said Max, bewildered.

The Eldest Girl nodded.

"What are you . . . ?" Max fumbled for the words. "You're not . . ."

"A ghost?" Emilie smoothed her cloak. "No. And I trust you two aren't, either?"

"Uh, no."

"Good. That's settled, at least. Now, Lukas, would you mind putting away that ridiculous sword before you accidentally run someone through?"

Lukas was grinning as he sheathed his sword, but then his expression turned serious. "Emilie, you're supposed to be looking after New Hamelin, not following us."

"Pish. Finn has the defense of the village well in hand. And who's to say that I was following you? Frankly, I'm as surprised to see you here as you are to see me."

At that moment there was a loud thud from downstairs, followed by the squeaking of floorboards as someone pounded up the steps. Someone heavy.

Lukas's hand flew to his sword, but Emilie shook her head. "Calm yourself, Lukas. It's a friend."

A massive figure appeared in the doorway, with a stack of freshly cut firewood balanced in his powerful arms. "Think I found enough to last us for the night," he called.

"Harold?" asked Max. "You, too?"

"Huh?" The trollson's face peeked out from behind the stack of firewood. "Oh! Max!" He tossed the firewood aside and grabbed Max in a massive hug. "Hey, and Lukas!" Just as quickly he pulled the other boy into the same embrace, one arm per person.

"It's Max and Lukas, Emilie! Isn't that great? Wow, uh . . ." As Harold let Lukas and Max go, he looked from Emilie to the two of them and back again, noticing the disapproving frowns all around. "So, why am I the only one in the room who thinks this is cool?"

Max planted her hands on her hips. "Emilie and Harold, what are you two doing in Shades Harbor?"

"Oh, about that . . . Emilie, are you gonna tell them?"

Max turned to the girl, waiting for an explanation. For once, Emilie didn't meet her stare. The girl's eyes drifted to the floor, to the hearth, anyplace but her friends. That's when Max saw that those blue eyes of hers weren't exactly as she remembered. They were bloodshot and puffy. Tired eyes. Or sad.

"We left soon after the two of you set out," said Emilie. "Hours actually. We crossed the river shallows north of the Shimmering Forest and followed the western shore. And I say 'we' because Harold here followed me and wouldn't turn back. Turns out that trollsons are as stubborn as stone itself."

Harold blushed, but when Emilie said the words, she gave him a small smile.

"And it turns out I've been glad of the company. Though I'm perfectly capable of looking after myself."

Max remembered days spent building their raft. All the while, Emilie and Harold were steadily making their way south to Shades Harbor.

"Mrs. Amsel's going to really let us have it when we get back," said Harold. "We didn't tell her we were leaving New Hamelin, and—well, I'm not looking forward at all to what she'll say."

Lukas wandered over to the window. He picked up the candle and glanced outside. "Emilie, what *are* you doing here?"

"I . . . I came here . . ." Then all at once Emilie's stiff spine failed her. Her shoulders sagged and she collapsed into her chair. She turned away so that the others wouldn't be able to see her tears.

Harold explained, "She's looking for Paul."

"But Paul's . . ." Max found that she couldn't say the word *dead*. But there was no need because it was now suddenly, blindingly obvious why Emilie had come to Shades Harbor. Shades Harbor was a village of ghosts, after all, and what if one of those ghosts was Paul?

Lukas gave Harold a questioning look, but the boy giant shook his head. "We've been here since yesterday evening. We've kept a candle lit in the window for him, but so far, nothing."

Poor Emilie. Having lived for centuries thinking only about her responsibilities as Eldest Girl, she'd just recently allowed her guard down. And that had been because of a reckless, thickheaded prankster named Paul. Max knew that the girl missed him terribly, but she hadn't guessed just how much. If the shoe had been on the other foot, Emilie would have given Max such a lecture: *Foolish to put yourself into such danger! And what were you thinking, heading off into the wild by yourself? And to Shades Harbor of all places, you silly girl!*

But Max wasn't Emilie. She went to the girl and put her arms around her instead.

"I miss him, too," she whispered. "We all do." Then she let Emilie cry into her shoulder, even as she wiped away her own tears.

❧ CHAPTER FOUR ❧

The Piper's plan was to follow the coast south to Magician's Landing, stopping at times along the way for Carter's magic lessons. Hopefully this would keep them far from pursuing elves and wandering ogres. Today they'd meandered out to one of the pebbly beaches, where a line of sea stone formed a natural wave breaker. The rough Sea of Troubles still churned, but closer to shore the water had become a placid lagoon, and stranger still, the air here felt much warmer, and several yards of snow-free beach surrounded the lagoon.

As Carter followed the Piper down to the shore, he remarked on the strangeness of it all. "It's like a little pocket of summer all hidden away. The water looks warm enough to swim in!"

The Piper smirked. "That's what they're hoping you'll think."

"Who?"

"Since conjuring pies has been such a miserable failure, I thought we'd try a different tack for today's lesson." The Piper winked at him. "Let's annoy some mermaids."

From the little Carter knew of Summer Isle mermaids, they liked to lure males into the sea to be drowned. Annoying them didn't sound like a good idea.

"Now, if you find a swimming hole that looks too perfect to be true, that's a sure sign that mermaids are lying in wait nearby," said the Piper. "Ages ago a school of them tried to use their song to lure me into the sea, but I turned the tables and played my own siren song on them. It took them days to drag themselves back out to sea!" The Piper chuckled at the memory. "We haven't really been friendly since, so I'm going to hide while you get their attention."

"Wait, how do I do that?"

"Just walk up and down the shore for a while. I'm sure they'll spot you even if you can't see them yet."

"Then what?" This already sounded like a terrible idea. They were going fishing with Carter as bait.

But the Piper shrugged with impatience. "The mermaids will sing and try to lure you into the water, of course. But this is where the lesson in magic comes in."

Carter waited for the Piper to continue, but the young man just watched him, expectantly.

"Well?" said Carter.

"Well what?"

"What's the lesson?"

"Don't listen, of course! If you do, you're dead."

Carter threw up his hands. "So I stuff my ears with cotton or something? What's the point?"

"No, no," said the Piper, shaking his head. "Not like that. Don't try to not hear the song—don't hear the magic."

"I don't understand." As usual, the Piper was acting like this was all the simplest, most obvious stuff in the world.

With a deep sigh, the Piper said, "The mermaid songs are just music, and music can't hurt you. It's not dangerous at all."

"But you said—"

"It's the magic beneath the music that's dangerous. The siren song carries the magic, like leaves on the wind. The trick, then, is to hear the music but resist the magic."

"Okay, and how do I do that?"

The Piper thumped Carter on the forehead. "Focus."

"Ow! Cut it out already."

"You almost got eaten by an ogre because you couldn't focus. I haven't had a decent slice of pie in weeks because you can't focus." The Piper gestured to the calm, gray water. "In there somewhere are creatures that will lead you to your death if you don't focus. When they start to sing, clear your head of useless thoughts. See what the magic is trying to do, how it's trying to take random chance and make it into a certainty. Break that certainty. Defend yourself against the magic."

Carter had never been much of a swimmer back home, and drowning seemed like a particularly bad way to go. So lonely. But unlike summoning pies, this actually would be useful if he could manage it. Protecting himself against magic had to be one of the most important things he could learn. Especially magic based in music. Like the Piper's.

"Okay." Carter breathed deep. "So if I successfully resist their magic, then what?"

The Piper grinned wide. His eyes practically glittered with mischief. "Then we get to watch mermaids throw a huge temper tantrum. See? Fun!"

"And if I fail? Will you save me?"

The Piper's face fell. "Less fun, but yes. If I absolutely have to."

The Piper hid himself in a outcropping of rocks near the far end of the lagoon. Close enough to see, but hopefully far enough away from Carter to not be seen.

"Right," said Carter. "I can do this." Somewhat haltingly, he put one foot in front of the other until he was at the water's edge. The gentle waves tried to lap at his feet, but he made sure to keep his toes dry. He waited and nothing happened. The lagoon remained calm, the water's surface unbroken by so much as a minnow.

After a few minutes Carter peered over to the outcropping where the Piper had hidden himself. He could just see the Piper crouched against the landward side of the rocks. His garishly checkered cloak made for poor camouflage against the dark sea stone, but hopefully it wasn't visible from the water. Carter shrugged at him, and the Piper made a walking gesture with his fingers. So Carter began walking up and down the beach, whistling to himself as if he were just a boy out for stroll along the seashore.

If no mermaids appeared, no doubt the Piper would find a way to blame it on Carter.

Carter heard a sudden splash and turned in time to see the tip of a large fin disappearing beneath the water. Something had just surfaced and quickly dived down again. His hands began to sweat with nervousness, but Carter tried to keep walking casually. Then, not more than twenty or thirty feet out, several heads appeared. Once, when Carter was journeying with Lukas and the others, he'd seen mermaids, but that had been from a distance. Now he could clearly see their scaly faces and toothy grins. Only their hair was beautiful—shining strands of gold and red.

Carter was reminded of the anglerfish, with its one shiny bauble designed to attract prey. There was no way he was going anywhere near them.

But then they started to sing. A chorus of voices, sweet and seductive. The words were unimportant, but the melody filled his heart with longing. He wanted—no, he *needed* to be out there with them, playing in the waves.

The music was everywhere. The Piper had told him to focus, to clear his head of unnecessary things, but the music wasn't unnecessary—it was vital. He had to obey.

One step into the water. Two. The water, it turned out, wasn't warm at all, but ice cold. For some reason Carter didn't mind.

But then the music suddenly became discordant as another song began to drown the mermaids' out. The gentle notes of a flute tried to coax Carter back onto shore, back to safety. Carter was caught between two battling songs, two powerful magics fighting to command his actions. He put his hands over his ears, but it wasn't enough.

Then he saw it. Even with his eyes closed, he saw the

lines of magic vibrating in the air all around him. The Piper was right: there was nothing special about the music; it was what the music was doing to the magic—manipulating it. Manipulating Carter.

The magic was thrumming all around him, and Carter reached out his fingers to quiet the strings.

All at once, his head cleared. He was standing hip-deep in freezing cold water, which he felt acutely, but he was no longer under the control of the mermaids or the Piper. They were still singing, and the Piper was still playing—Carter could see him standing on the outcropping, his cloak blowing in the wind. The music went on, but Carter had successfully freed himself from both spells. He'd defended himself.

Carter pulled himself out of the water, and as he did so, the mermaids' song turned shrill. He didn't stop until he reached dry land, even though each step stuck pins and needles into his toes, frozen from the ice water.

"I did it!" Carter cried.

But the Piper was still too busy playing to hear him. Just as he was too busy playing to see the pair of mermaids rising up from the water behind him. They held a net woven of seaweed and kelp and were preparing to use it to snare the Piper.

Carter shouted for the Piper to look out, but the mermaids in the sea drowned out his words with their singing. Carter tried to summon a wind like he'd seen the Piper do, to blow the mermaids back into the sea. He reached for the magic, but the strings slipped from his fingers. He was panicking too much to keep his fingers steady.

The net came down on the Piper, abruptly cutting off

his song. With a shriek of triumph the mermaids threw themselves upon him, dragging him into the water.

Carter ran. He didn't have the magic at that moment, but for once he did have two perfectly good legs. He bounded across the beach, snatching up a nice, club-sized piece of driftwood. He reached the rocks just as the mermaids were pulling the struggling Piper away from the shore.

They bared their teeth and hissed when they saw him, but they didn't look half as fearsome in shallow water. Just two beached fish.

The mermaids retreated from Carter's club, letting go of the Piper and escaping out to sea. Then Carter helped the Piper untangle himself from the net, and waited for the Piper's verbal lashing. Carter had failed at first to resist the mermaids' song. Carter hadn't been focused. Carter had very nearly gotten the Piper killed.

Instead, the Piper surprised him by throwing his arms around him. At first, Carter thought the Piper was crying, but he soon realized that those sobs were actually laughter. Dumbfounded, Carter pulled himself free.

"That was brilliant!" the Piper cried. Then he spun Carter around and pointed to the lagoon. There, five mermaids were thrashing about in the water, spitting and cursing and pulling their hair. "Just look at them." The Piper turned a beaming grin back to Carter. "And you thought this wouldn't be any fun!"

CHAPTER FIVE

At least the evening promised to be warm and dry. Harold built up the fire in the hearth until it was roaring, and soon the room was toasty. Max and Lukas didn't like the idea of spending the night in Shades Harbor, but Emilie was set on staying until morning. She'd sat in that window holding vigil for Paul's spirit for a whole day, and she would wait a few hours more, at least. After much arguing, Lukas was able to make Emilie promise that if Paul didn't appear by dawn, she'd go with Harold back to New Hamelin. In the meantime, they agreed to take turns at the window, so that Emilie might get some rest. They were, all of them, haggard and tired. If they pushed themselves much further, they would begin to resemble shades themselves.

It was Max's turn to watch at the window. She put a

fresh log on the fire, and a fresh candle on the windowsill, which by then was stained white with wax drippings. Shades Harbor by moonlight looked even lonelier than before. As the sun had set, the hanging lanterns along the waterfront were lit, although Max never did see who lit them. The lanterns glowed pale and cold, and hardly seemed to turn back the darkness at all.

"Ghost lamps."

Max started and turned to see Emilie standing behind her.

"Sorry, I didn't mean to scare you."

"You didn't, much." Max wrapped her cloak tight around her. There was a chill about Shades Harbor that had nothing to do with the cold. "You should be asleep."

"I've slept enough. Can I join you for a while?"

Max nodded as Emilie drew up a seat. The girl was careful not to wake Harold or Lukas as she scooted the chair legs closer to the window.

"Why'd you call them ghost lamps?" asked Max. "I mean, besides the obvious, that we're in ghost central."

"The lanterns' sole purpose is to guide in the black ships looking for safe harbor. See there? There's another."

Max cupped her hands over her eyes and pressed her face to the window. Silver lights lined the shore. "Like lighthouses, right?"

"Yes. Only, because of the ice, I don't think the ships can come or go. They're stranded here along with everyone else."

"Everyone? You mean . . ."

Emilie arched an eyebrow at her. "Yes, the ghosts. Did you feel them as you walked through the village? Hundreds of them."

Max remembered the feeling on the docks, of being jostled and shoved by invisible hands. It was as if the docks were overcrowded with spirits waiting for something. Maybe it was the missing ships. "So what do you think that means? If the ships stop coming and going?"

"Nothing good. But then again, nothing good has come from this awful winter. I fear the Summer Isle is broken in ways we don't even understand yet, with consequences far graver than ice and snow."

She laid her forehead against the windowpane and closed her eyes. "Listen to me go on. If Paul were here, he'd say something, do something that would make it impossible to despair. It's moments like this I miss him the most."

Max understood, or thought she did. There had been enough times that she'd expected to hear Carter's voice, or wished that she could look up and see her mom and dad smiling back at her. But Max still had the chance to get them all back, to find Carter and break her parents' curse. Paul was dead and there was no changing that, even on the Summer Isle. Yet Max would stay at the window and keep watch, for Emilie.

Just in case.

"You knew we'd try to stop you from coming here," said Max. "That's why you waited until we were gone. You didn't even mention it."

Emilie gave a tired shrug. "If someone else had come to me with the same plan, I'd have tied them up and locked them in the pigsty for their foolishness. It's an irresponsible, irrational thing to do."

"And yet here you are."

"With Paul, being rational was never much use."

Max nodded. That was one of the truest things Emilie had ever said. "Nice pants, by the way."

Emilie looked down at her trousers and smiled. "After some adjustments, they fit nicely. To tell you the truth, I think I may be done with skirts altogether."

Max chuckled. If nothing else, she had brought a little modern thinking to the Summer Isle. Win or lose, she could be proud of that.

Minutes stretched into an hour, into two. The moon drifted across the sky until it was no longer visible outside the window. Max was getting ready to tell Emilie, for the fourth time, to go back to bed when she caught a glimpse of movement down by the dock. She sat up straight.

Emilie noticed the sudden change in posture. "What is it?"

"I don't know," answered Max. "Thought I saw something, but . . . Wait, there. Look!"

A figure had stepped out of the darkness into the glow of the ghost lamps. He seemed to be watching the window.

"Paul?" Emilie whispered, but the figure was too far away and too dark still for Max to know for sure.

"We'd better wake the others—"

Max's words were cut off by Emilie's sharp intake of breath. Another figure had appeared in the dark. And another. Soon the dock was filled with people, hundreds of them, crowded together beneath the ghost lamps. Max could see the faces of those nearest the inn—men, women and children. But pale and indistinct, like a picture slightly out of focus.

Lost spirits. The ghosts of Shades Harbor, and they were, all of them, staring up at Max and Emilie in the window.

The odd chill in the room they'd been battling all night turned frigid, and Max could see her breath in front of her face, despite the fire still burning in the hearth.

"Lukas! Harold!"

The two boys started awake. "What happened?" gasped Lukas. "It's freezing in here!"

Max pointed to the outside. "I think we're in trouble."

Lukas strapped on his sword as he joined them at the window. "Oh, no."

"Wow, that's a lot of ghosts," breathed Harold. "How long have they been out there?"

"Just a few minutes," answered Emilie. "That we could see, anyway. At first it was just one, and I'd hoped . . . I'd thought . . ." The girl swallowed her own words and looked away. "So foolish. I've put us all in danger."

"This is the Summer Isle," said Max. "When are we not in danger?"

"They're just looking at us." Harold went to the window and gave a tentative wave hello.

"Will you cut that out?" snapped Max. Harold clearly did not have nearly enough experience dealing with the dead.

"Well, they're not attacking us, or whatever," he said. "Maybe they're curious."

Lukas scratched his chin. "The last time we visited this

place, the ghosts barely even acknowledged we were there. I wonder what's changed."

"Emilie has a theory about that," said Max. "Don't you, Emilie?"

The Eldest Girl smoothed her cloak and sat up straight. She seemed her old self again. "An observation, more than a theory. If the black ships have stopped coming and going, then Shades Harbor stops being a waypoint; it becomes more like a prison. Those ghosts might be trapped here."

"And prisoners are rarely happy about being in prison," said Lukas. "So we're looking at, what, a couple hundred angry ghosts? I sure hope they're content with glaring at us."

"Uh, guys?" Harold tapped on the glass with a thick finger. "Something's happening down there."

One by one the ghosts were stepping aside as they made way for a lone figure pushing his way through the crowd. Max felt Emilie stiffen by her side. The girl's hand found hers, and Max gave it a squeeze.

Please let it be Paul, for her sake.

But it wasn't. The ghost who made his way to the front, who was looking up at them now, was too old, too bald and too shrunken to be Paul, but Max knew him just the same.

His appearance was at once a bitter disappointment and a cause for hope. As she heard the others gasp, Max knew they were feeling much the same.

The Peddler had returned.

CHAPTER SIX

Lukas told the others to stay inside the inn, but of course no one listened. These days he often wondered how he'd ever managed to get the boys of the village Watch to obey his orders, but then the entire Watch couldn't hold a candle to the stubbornness of one pink-haired girl.

"At least stand behind me," he said to Max.

"Okay. But only because you've got that fancy anti-magic sword."

"I don't think that's exactly how it works."

"Whatever. I want one."

Harold and Emilie brought up the rear, and as the four companions stepped out into the night, they were hit with a wall of intense cold, far colder than a winter's night, but also waves of fear and anger. Raw emotions emanated from the ghosts with every lifeless breath—they exhaled danger. Any sane person would have run from a single menacing ghost, much less a hundred. But Lukas had spent countless nights on the walls of New Hamelin, face-first against the unknown. He'd grown accustomed to it.

He led the others cautiously toward the docks, which were lit by the eerie ghost lamps. There was nothing inviting about that sallow, unhealthy light.

The spirits of Shades Harbor made no sound as the children approached. When they got within twenty or so feet of the spectral crowd, Emilie whispered, "I think that's far enough, Lukas." He wholeheartedly agreed.

The shade at the front of the others stepped forward.

"Is that really you, Peddler?" Lukas asked.

"Yes, what there is of me."

If seeing him had been a shock, hearing the old magician's voice was all the more heartbreaking. The Peddler sounded hollow, like an echo. But he wore the same good-natured scowl that Lukas remembered.

"You're a ghost. We'd hoped . . ." Lukas found the words hard to say. "I hoped . . ."

"I died. Stings to say it out loud, but there it is."

"Peddler," said Emilie, her voice also tight. "Please, we're looking for someone."

The Peddler frowned. "He's not here, Emilie. I'm sorry."

Emilie's hands went to her mouth as Max slid an arm around her for support.

"You've already grieved for him once; don't grieve for him again," said the Peddler. "Paul's spirit isn't in Shades

Harbor because he died protecting those he loved. He's at peace. Trust me, his journey from here on out will be an easy one. The boy's earned it."

Lukas felt relieved to hear that much, but it hurt, too. He hadn't admitted just how much he'd wanted to see his friend again.

"Children," said the Peddler. "Do you think we could go inside and talk in front of the fire? I would . . . like that."

Lukas glanced worriedly at the restless crowd of shades.

But the Peddler gave a little wave. "You don't need to worry about them. I've explained that none of this is your fault."

"Of course not," said Max. "It's the Piper's!"

The Peddler shook his head. "No, my dear, it's mine. It's all mine."

For once, Max was speechless.

"I'll explain, inside. I promise."

This time Lukas let the Peddler lead the way, and he followed, a thousand questions swirling around in his head.

❖

By the light of their fireplace, Lukas marveled at the Peddler's ghost. The old man looked as he had in life, only . . . thin. Not in weight, but substance, like a spiderweb adrift on the wind. When he stood in front of the fireplace, the flames glowed through him, making him almost translucent. Lukas wondered what it would feel like to touch him, or if he could be touched at all.

If Carter had still been with them, he probably would

have tried; the boy was insatiably curious. But the young Captain of the Watch kept his hands to himself. Max and Emilie eyed the Peddler warily, and Harold could not stop his openmouthed staring. The cold that had settled in the room only grew worse. They wrapped blankets around themselves even as they sat in front of the fire.

The Peddler gazed into the flames. "I do miss a good, roaring fire. I cannot feel the heat, but looking helps me remember it. Ghost light chills the spirit as well as the flesh."

"Peddler," said Lukas. "Why are you here? You said that Paul had . . . moved on." Lukas stole a glance at Emilie, but the girl seemed to be holding herself together. "Why haven't you?"

The Peddler shook his head. "Stubbornness, I guess. My work's not yet done, but unfortunately I'm no longer alive to do it." He turned to take them all in, one at a time. "You see, children, I miscalculated. I didn't recognize how deep Yaga's plans went—as deep as the roots in that forest of hers. This isle is in terrible danger from the witch of the Bone-wood."

"Not just Grannie Yaga," said Max, folding her arms across her chest. "What about the Piper?"

"The Piper might be in the most danger of all," said the Peddler.

"Are you kidding?"

"This land is in peril. Your lives, and the lives of countless others, hang in the balance. But the Piper is in a battle for his soul."

Max didn't look like she believed it. "You know, the first time we met, you made me promise that if I ever got the chance to spare the Piper's life, I would. Since we've pretty much gotten our butts kicked from that point on, I don't see that happening anytime soon. What is it with you two, anyway?"

When the Peddler had been alive, he'd been guarded and cantankerous, and he'd dodged talk of the Piper. Lukas had observed him doing it many times. But in death, the Peddler had changed. The scowl had melted away, and in its place was something like regret.

"What was the Piper's greatest crime?" the Peddler asked.

"Bringing us here," Lukas answered for Max. "Stealing the children of Hamelin. Max and her brother."

"Yes, he took you from your homes, but what made the deed even more unforgivable was that he brought you all here to the Summer Isle. To the land of magic, a place never meant for mortal folk. It was always a place of spirit, and in time, a haven for beings born with magic in their veins. Like me. Like your friend Harold, there."

Some of Harold's ancestors had been trolls, so that very same magic gave this boy his enormous size and strength. It didn't, however, prevent the boy from blushing a deep crimson when the Peddler looked at him.

"Back in your world, magic is weak because the laws of the universe are strong. They keep it in check. Very little happens outside the boundaries of those laws, what you would call reality." The Peddler gave them a wink. "Which is good, because humans are beings of chaos. Children, especially. You can't help it. Oh, it's hidden away, because on the outside you're flesh and blood, bone and muscle. You are firmly rooted in the physical world; you obey its laws. But in here"—the Peddler pointed to Lukas's head—"in here, you're imagination and desires. Love and hate and joy and sorrow, all wrapped up together. Luminous! In short, you are all magical."

Lukas scratched his head. He didn't know what to think of all this. Back in old Hamelin, he knew Father Warner preached about souls, but he hadn't had much use for his since coming to the Summer Isle.

The Peddler continued. "You take a being like that, you set a human boy or girl loose in a place where anything is possible"—the Piper heaved a sigh—"well, you are inviting disaster."

"See?" said Max. "That's another reason to be mad at the Piper. He brought us all here in the first place, so if the Summer Isle is all out of whack, it's his fault."

"But the Piper wasn't the first person to allow a human child to walk on the shores of the Summer Isle. It was me."

Lukas didn't understand. Everyone knew the Piper had violated the laws of this land when he'd brought the children of Hamelin to the Summer Isle, and the Peddler and the Princess had joined forces to punish him for it.

The Peddler read the look of bewilderment on Lukas's face. "Understand, I was never one for talking about myself, but it's important for you to know what happened to the Piper, what went so terribly wrong despite the best of intentions.

"You see, there was a time long, long before recorded history, when this isle of magic and your world were not so far apart, and my kind, the immortals, could come and go as we pleased. We were never all that much different from you. We were all of us wise at times, stupid at others. Some of us, myself included, liked to mingle among the simpler creatures—the trolls, the elves, the kobolds—without drawing too much attention to ourselves. After all, who thinks twice of the old peddler wandering by? But there were others who relished hearing their names spoken with wonder. Or with fear."

"Grannie Yaga," said Emilie. "You're talking about the witch."

"Yes," agreed the Peddler. "Yaga was one of the worst. Clever and cruel, she developed appetites of which I'm sure you're all aware. But not even Yaga anticipated the tenacity of you mortals, or your ingenuity. In time, humans changed the world. You lit the dark places first with torches, then with lamps. You chopped down the ancient forests. You tamed the wild, and as the world grew smaller, my kind began to disappear."

"How?" asked Max. "If you're immortal, doesn't that mean you get to live forever?"

"Not always." The Peddler smiled. "I'm now proof of that. In any case, it became obvious that the days of the magical folk were numbered in your world, and the only way we would survive was to retreat to the magical isle of our birth and close the doors behind us. Sever the two worlds forever."

Lukas tried to put this information into perspective. He'd always assumed that the Peddler was some kind of ancient magician, but to hear him tell it, he was much more.

He'd been described once to Lukas as a force of nature, but Lukas had never been able to reconcile that description with the irascible old wanderer who liked to trade jokes.

"My problem was, I'd become fond of humans in general," said the Peddler. "And overly protective of one in particular. He was just a boy struggling to survive a harsh winter on his own. He and his mother had been banished from their home for some nonsense charges of witchcraft. The boy's mother was a midwife and good with herbs, but no witch. They'd wandered without a home, and what little food she managed to beg for she fed to the boy, until she succumbed to sickness and hunger."

The Peddler shook his head, his eyes lost in memory.

"When I first met him, he was a lad of fifteen, living on the streets, playing music for pennies. He was already quite good at it, but the other beggars—grown-ups mostly— would beat him and steal his earnings. Still, he managed to survive."

"That boy was the Piper?" asked Max.

The Peddler nodded. "He was smart. He was resourceful, but he was in need of rescuing and I thought . . . I should have known better. I was already past my time on earth. There was no place for me there anymore, but I'd spent so much time around humans, and I thought I could carry a little bit of humanity with me, in the form of this clever, needy young man. It wasn't the first mistake I'd ever made, but it was by far the gravest."

The Peddler turned from the fire and drifted to the window. Lukas followed his gaze. The shades now surrounded the inn. Silent and still, they stared up at the candle in the window. Waiting for what, Lukas didn't know.

"I knew from the moment we arrived what a mistake I'd made in bringing him here. No human had ever set foot on the Summer Isle, and for good reason. Your kind have a talent for changing your environment, and not always for the better. I was amazed at how quickly he learned. With the flute that had once belonged to his mother, he used his music to conjure magic! He was hungry to learn, and teaching him was my second-greatest mistake."

Max sniffed. "Sounds to me like all you did was try and help him. You didn't know what he'd do. It was his choice to become a villain."

"Was it?" asked the Peddler. "He wasn't like he is now. He may look young, but he's centuries old. Back then, he was still more boy on the inside than young man—a boy who'd been wounded, who'd had everything he loved stolen from him. And on the Summer Isle, evil is always whispering in your ear, as it is everywhere."

"Grannie Yaga, you mean," said Lukas.

"I didn't realize it until it was too late. You see, Yaga was loath to leave her dark forests back in the old world. She'd always meddled in the affairs of humans when it suited her. Hunted them when it didn't. A terrible creature. A predator through and through.

"When she finally fled to the Summer Isle, it was like putting a wolf in a cage. She claimed the Bonewood as her own, but she longed for what she'd lost. By bringing the Piper here, I gave her the means to get it back.

"The doors between worlds were supposed to lock behind us, but the Piper found a way to open them again. Children will surprise you."

"So was it the Piper's idea to kidnap us," asked Emilie, "or was it Grannie Yaga's?"

"Grannie planted the seed in the Piper's ear. What a way to have his revenge on the villagers who'd banished him! Steal their young from them! Why, he'd be doing the poor children a favor, saving them just as I'd saved him. But I'm sure Grannie never told him what she really wanted the children for."

Lukas and the others exchanged looks. They all knew the stories of Yaga's oven.

"A whole village of children to do with as she wished," said the Peddler. "There was only one problem: like I said, Grannie had a vision of the future, and that vision spelled trouble for the old witch."

"That's where the prophecy came from," said Lukas. *"Only when the last son of Hamelin appears and the Black Tower found will the Piper's prison open and the children return safe and sound."*

"No sooner had she put her plan in motion to steal the children of Hamelin, than she received a prophecy detailing their salvation!" The Peddler chuckled. "Must've sent her into quite a fury."

"But the prophecy lied," said Lukas.

"Did it?" asked the Peddler. "Carter freed the Piper. Max opened a door that could not be opened. There's magic at work in the Weber siblings—you can't deny it."

Max took Lukas's hand. "Are you saying that Carter

might still fulfill the rest of the prophecy? That he could lead the children home again?"

"Grannie Yaga certainly thinks so," said the Peddler. "Why else would the witch spend her time looking for him, when by all other accounts she's already won?"

Lukas looked around at his friends' faces. They'd dared to hope so many times, and had been met with bitter disappointment each and every time. Emilie wore her skepticism openly, as he knew she would, but to Lukas's surprise, Max looked troubled.

"Max?"

"She wants to kill him," said Max quietly. "Grannie thinks it's the only way to keep the rest of the prophecy from coming true."

"I'm sorry," said the Peddler. "But I fear you're right. Carter was valuable to her when she needed him to free the Piper, but now he's a danger to her plans."

"She won't stop with us," said Lukas. "She'll use the Piper to bring more children to the Summer Isle. He already threatened to steal them away one by one."

The Peddler pointed to the night sky outside their window. "And they would wake up in a land of eternal dark, Yaga's personal hunting ground. That's her plan, has been all along. Free the Piper and use him to supply her with children for eternity."

"He would do that?" asked Emilie. "Is he so wicked?"

"I hope not. I pray that there's a glimmer inside him of the boy I once knew. But to tell you the truth, I don't know him anymore. Grannie twisted his brain with all her lies.

She is a master of manipulation, and I don't know how far her poison has spread."

Max pulled away from Lukas, her eyes wet with tears as she pointed at the Peddler. "You started all this! Help us!"

"I wish I could. But I can't leave this harbor, and even if I could, I'm only a shade now—my magic died with me. There is still hope, though, because despite the witch's many servants, she has not been able to find Carter. Someone is hiding him from her. Perhaps unknowingly, but someone has been helping us."

"The Princess?" asked Harold. Everyone looked at him in surprise. "What? I've been paying attention, that's all."

"Perhaps," said the Peddler slowly. "There's more to the Princess than I'm at liberty to tell, but I've got a feeling that her part in this story isn't over yet. In any case, you should go soon, the morning at the latest. Carter won't stay hidden from the witch forever."

"Nothing's changed," Lukas said. "We have to find Carter. And if Grannie Yaga tries to stop us . . ." Lukas drew the Sword of the Eldest Boy. He'd disliked the thing from the first day it'd been presented to him. Disliked what it stood for, the responsibility it conferred. Long, long ago, the Peddler had gifted it to the original Eldest Boy, Marc. Then when Marc had disappeared, it went to Leon. Now both boys were slaves of the rat king, along with all the other children who'd been lost over the many years. Those boys had been older and wiser than Lukas, and he'd never felt worthy to hold the sword in their stead. He'd even tried to give it away.

For once, however, he would relish using it, if it meant chopping Grannie's head from her wrinkled neck. Vengeance for Paul, if nothing else.

The Peddler seemed to guess what was in Lukas's heart. "Be careful," the old magician said. "That old sword has a dark history, from the time when humans hunted my kind. It was forged for one purpose—to kill creatures of magic. It's too long a story to tell how it came into my possession, but I gave it to you in the hope that it might be put to good use for a change. The sword may well be needed, but vengeance is a dangerous path. Look where it led the Piper."

"I'm not like him," said Lukas.

"Neither was he, once upon a time." The Peddler drifted back to the window. Slowly, he reached out to touch the candle's flame. His hand passed through it, unharmed. Then he left his hand in the flame, not hurting. Not feeling. "I'm sorry to leave this burden to you, children. You must win the war I started. But heed the warning of the Piper's example, Lukas. Save Carter. Lead your people home again. And leave vengeance for a higher power."

CHAPTER SEVEN

To stay clear of the elves' forest, the Piper insisted that they continue south along the coast. This wouldn't have been such a bad thing if the Summer Isle's eastern shore had been all sandy beaches, but the coastline was made up of rocky crags and steep drops. The Piper seemed to revel in every misstep that Carter took, every perilous drop that Carter barely avoided. The Piper danced along the bluffs fearlessly, at times taunting Carter for his caution.

Carter wished the Piper would fall on his pied butt.

It was slow going, picking their way through the treacherous cliffs. Eventually the Piper was forced to carry Carter's pack for him just so the boy could keep up. Carter started to feel like he was merely a collection of scrapes and bruises, but that pain was nothing compared to the worry gnawing away at his gut. He still had no plan, no idea what to do when they finally reached that far-off spot known as

Magician's Landing. From the highest cliffs, they could see a lighthouse in the distance, a towering spire of rock built atop an islet. Now that they were closer, Carter could tell that what he'd mistakenly thought to be a narrow isthmus was actually a massive bridge, at least a mile long, that connected the lighthouse to the shore. Carter could only imagine the hands that had built such a structure. Beneath it all, the rough waters of the Sea of Troubles churned restlessly. They stopped to rest within view of the imposing sight.

"There are two ways onto Magician's Landing," said the Piper. "One by sea and one by land." The Piper eyed his work as he put the finishing touches on a new flute carved from driftwood.

"So we're going in by land, right?" asked Carter.

"Unless you're hiding a boat in one of your pockets, then we'll have to. And I doubt it gets any easier."

"You mean you haven't gone this way before?"

The Piper gave an impatient sigh and looked up from his work. "The Peddler and I came to the Summer Isle by ship. Magician's Landing is where we ran ashore, and that's how it got its name—haven't I told you all this before?"

"Actually, no. You told me that you two used to be friends, but that's it."

"Hmm. Well, the Peddler recognized my talent early on. Even though I was little more than an orphaned gutter rat, he knew that I had a way with song. And a way to make things happen with music. I'd already learned truths about the world that most folk scoffed at."

"Because of your mother."

The Piper nodded.

Carter knew that the villagers in Hamelin had accused the Piper and his mother of witchcraft, but he didn't want to linger on that too much. Any information the Piper shared with him could be useful later on, and talking too much about his mother usually caused the Piper to clam up. Or fly into a rage. Best to move on. "So the Peddler found you when you were living on your own?"

"I stayed alive by playing for my supper and by petty thievery. Little more than stealing pies off bakers' window-sills, but the Peddler noticed. He took me in. Fed me, gave me a home. But it couldn't last because he was getting ready to leave the old world for a new one. Because though he looked like a person, he wasn't really. I think I knew that, even from the first. The Peddler wasn't a man; he was . . . the Peddler, and he didn't belong among humans anymore."

The Piper scratched his chin.

"I begged and begged until he agreed to take me with him, but do you know, after he said yes, all I could think about was whether or not that ship would sink? I had night-mares about it. I'd never been on a ship. Never even seen much more than a rowboat. And of course I couldn't swim. Never mind the magic; for days we traveled together toward the coast, and every night I cried myself to sleep because I was afraid we'd drown."

"Did the Peddler know you were that scared?" Carter asked.

"He figured it out. He started offering a sweet every night before bed. Don't know where they came from, somewhere in that ridiculous backpack of his. Honey cakes, brandy sugar. He said that they were proof against bad dreams."

"Did it work? Did the nightmares stop?"

The Piper smiled. "No. But I didn't tell him that. I liked the candy too much."

He was quiet as he stared off into his memories.

"I know what you're thinking," he said after a moment. "You wonder if I miss him. Well, one happy memory doesn't change how I felt about that old magician. In the end, I was glad to be free of him. Always telling me what to do, always lecturing me. Good riddance."

The Piper wiped something from his eye. Maybe a tear. Maybe just a fleck of dust. Carter didn't ask.

Then the Piper shook himself and lifted his new flute to his lips. He played a little tune, barely more than a scale.

"There," said the Piper, admiring his handicraft. "Works."

Carter wanted to keep him talking. He wanted to know what exactly had happened when the pair reached the Summer Isle and how two close friends could become such enemies. But he didn't get the chance, because the Piper leaped to his feet. "We're making terrible time. Let's get going!"

"If I try to go any faster on the cliffs, I'm going to fall and split my head open."

The Piper scowled at him and walked to the far side of the cliff. There he stopped and stared across the valley, toward the Deep Forest's wall of green that dominated the western horizon. The Piper studied the landscape for a moment before calling Carter to his side.

Carter joined the Piper, who was pointing to the narrow trail barely visible in the distance. "There," he said.

People were climbing the trail. Four, five . . . six of them that Carter could see. Their earth-toned skin and tree-bark armor camouflaged them well, but he could still make out the bows strung loosely across their backs and the curved knives glinting in the daylight. Elves.

"They're hunting us." The Piper drew his pipe. "I had hoped they'd give up after we left the Deep Forest, but obviously not. You're lucky I finished this in time."

Carter held up a hand. "Me? They're after you, aren't they?"

"You helped me escape. I don't think they'll take kindly to that. But don't worry. There's nowhere for them to hide, so I think conjuring a simple rockslide will do the trick."

"Wait a minute: you can't kill them!"

"Us against them, Carter. Remember?" The Piper lifted his flute. "They'll drag us back in chains if we're lucky. Probably just behead us on the spot."

"Just stop it! I won't let you kill anyone."

The Piper actually laughed at him. "What are you going to do about it?"

"I'll . . . I'll leave. You'll have to go on alone."

There was a pause then. "So leave. Why should I care?"

Carter steeled himself for this next part. "You care. And it's not just because you think I can help you get your pipe back."

"Really?"

"You don't like to be alone. Can't say I blame you after all those years in that tower by yourself. But it's not just the tower. After your mom died, you were alone then, too. Alone and afraid. I . . . I think it made you angry, and that's why you keep doing the things you do. But you don't have to keep doing them. You can change."

There was a tense moment when the Piper said nothing. When he finally did answer, his voice was little more than a whisper. "You pity me, don't you? The Peddler pitied me, too, you know."

"No one else has to die. No one has to get hur—"

The Piper cut Carter off by snatching the front of his collar so fast that Carter didn't have time even to react. "Listen to me, *apprentice*. You don't know me. A few stories and a couple of weeks traveling together, and you think you understand me? I'm centuries old! I'm the greatest magician *ever,* and you"—with a snarl he shoved Carter, roughly, to the ground—"*you* will learn your place!" The Piper stepped over Carter. "Until then, stay out of my way."

Then, in one fluid motion, he brought his pipe to his lips and blew a new tune. This one was harsher than before, discordant and ugly.

Carter heard a distant rumble. So near the cliff's edge, he had a good view of the elves on the trail below, and of the tons of rock precariously hanging over their heads. A sudden, piercing crack echoed out across the valley as the Piper's spell split rock and earth. The elves looked worriedly about them, searching for the source of the fearful noise. Then they began to run in the opposite direction, down the path, but Carter feared they wouldn't be fast enough.

He couldn't sit by and watch as the Piper buried them beneath a mountain. Carter scrambled to his feet and threw himself at the Piper. He tried to tackle him around the middle, like he'd seen football players do, but Carter was a good deal shorter than the Piper and slammed into his legs instead.

Though the Piper managed to stay on his feet, his song was interrupted as he spun around and tried to untangle himself from Carter's grasp. The song was cut short, but an ominous rumble remained.

"Get off me!" The Piper backhanded Carter, catching him across the jaw.

Lights exploded in Carter's vision, and he lost his grip on the magician.

As Carter rubbed his eyes to clear his sight, the Piper leaped away, landing atop a boulder on the edge of the bluff. He took up his song again, and there was another terrifying rumble as rocks and dirt began to rain onto the trail below. Carter could no longer see the elves.

"Stop!" cried Carter, and instinctively he reached out his hand toward the Piper. He didn't know what he was doing, exactly, only that the Piper needed to be stopped before he buried the elves. What if Leetha was down there with them? The elf girl's face burned bright in Carter's mind. Her wry smile. The look of hurt when he'd betrayed her to save the Piper.

The Piper changed his tune to a lullaby, and Carter felt all the fight start to drain out of him. The music filled him up and made his arms and legs heavy. He might as well lie down right there and sleep. Sleep . . .

No. Carter shook off the sleep. He cut off the magic just like he had with the mermaids. Just as the Piper had taught him to.

Carter straightened up and put himself between the Piper and the cliff. "No more," he said. "No more."

The Piper's eyes went wide with surprise, then narrowed

again in anger. "You . . . d-dare!" he sputtered, his face turning red.

Carter braced himself as the Piper blew a single, piercing note. Carter actually felt the magic wash over him, a wave of power emanating from the Piper's pipe. But then there was another crack, this one quieter than the splitting of rock and stone. Unable to safely channel that much power, the Piper's driftwood flute snapped to pieces in his hands.

The Piper began to panic as he lost his hold on the spell, and the magic went wild. Possibilities ran unchecked, uncontrolled. The earth split open wide, and the cliff vanished in a sudden explosion. Somewhere the Piper called out Carter's name.

Then Carter fell, and he kept falling.

CHAPTER EIGHT

"Max, we're going to be late!"

Carter pressed his ear to his sister's door. Drawers opened, drawers closed. But the bedroom door stayed locked.

He knocked again, and still there was no answer.

"Mom! Can you tell her to hurry up? We're going to miss the movie!"

Carter's mom peeked around the hallway. She was still wearing the reading glasses that made her look bug-eyed. "Maxine? Time to go."

"I'm coming," said a voice from inside. The lock clicked and the door swung open. Max was wearing her jeans, big black combat boots and an anime T-shirt. Exactly the same clothing she'd had on when she went inside to change.

Max took one look at Carter's outfit, however, and said,

"What? No way. I am not going anywhere with you dressed like that."

"Oh, come on!"

"What are those things on your head supposed to be? Green ears? And are you wearing . . ."

"Dad's bathrobe." Carter opened his arms and let the sleeves drape low. "It's too big, but it works."

"You look hilarious. And not in a good way."

"This is the kind of movie where people dress up," said Carter. "Especially on opening day, so can we please just go?"

Max crossed her arms in front of her chest and didn't budge. "Not like that. Ditch the ears."

"No way! Without the ears I'm just a kid in a big bathrobe."

"I'm not going out in public with the king of the nerds!"

Their mom yanked her glasses off. "Enough! Both of you, I have work to do here, so please, please, stop fighting and give me some peace!" She reached into her pocket and pulled out a wad of cash. "Here, you can get yourselves one of those disgusting mountain-sized popcorns. Just leave! Please?"

Carter and Max exchanged a look. Their mom was kind of a nut about trans fats and those sorts of things, so in the Weber household when you were offered the rare chance to eat something really unhealthy, you took it. No questions asked.

Max snatched up the money and headed for the front door. "Okay, but if anyone asks who the green-eared little freak is, I'll pretend like I don't know you."

"No one will ask, because it's obvious to the ninety-nine

percent of the population who've actually seen the other Star Wars movies—" Carter stumbled. The plastic-and-metal brace that supported his left leg brushed the coffee table and caught on a protruding screw. Carter nearly fell headfirst into it. Max was there to catch him, though, quick as lightning.

Their mother rushed to his side. "Carter, honey, are you all right?"

"Yeah," he said, rubbing his leg. "I'm fine."

Max helped him steady himself. "I thought Dad said he was going to do something about that screw. I gouged my shin on that thing last week."

Max was fibbing, of course. She'd never gouged her shin, and the table certainly wasn't to blame for Carter's fall. But ever since the last operation had failed to fix his twisted foot, Carter's family had started talking around his disability. Ignoring it. Before the operation, it had been easy to face it head-on, like an opponent they were all training to fight. But the match was over, the operation a failure and Carter still the boy with the limp.

Their mom sighed. "I'll remind your father about that table. *Again*. But, Carter, are you sure you're okay? Maybe you two should use that popcorn money to take a cab instead."

Uh-oh. No way was Carter going to give up his well-earned portion of salt and butter flavoring, not because of a stupid stumble over a piece of furniture. "Mom, I'm fine! The subway's good. Max'll watch out for me."

"Yeah," said Max. "Subway's a lot less treacherous than our living room."

They quickly waved goodbye and scooted out the door before their mom could press the issue any further. As they waited for the building elevator, Carter wiped his brow. "Whew, close call."

"Yeah, she who giveth popcorn taketh away."

Carter grinned. "Thanks for the catch, by the way."

His sister shrugged it off, but she was smiling, too. "Anytime. I'll always have your back—you know that. Now take off the ears."

❖

When Carter opened his eyes, he wasn't sure what he was looking at. It definitely wasn't his sister. A white-and-brown blur, and in the middle of that blur, a bird looking down at him, head cocked and curious. When Carter licked his lips, he tasted grit, and only then did he realize that the white blur was snow, the brown was dirt. The world was slowly coming into focus. The bird was a seagull, and it watched him, pausing only now and again to clean its feathers.

Carter had fallen. He remembered the fight with the Piper atop the cliff, the ground giving way beneath him. Somehow, Carter had survived the fall, but where was he now?

When Carter shifted his weight to get a better look at his surroundings, a biting pain shot from his ankle up his leg. The hurt was so strong that Carter cried out, scaring the seagull into flight. A wave of nausea roiled up from his stomach, and he laid his head back down, afraid he was going to be sick. Only after the feeling had passed did Carter dare look down at his leg.

His pants were torn, dirty, and stained with clotted blood. His ankle felt as if it were on fire—the ankle he'd kept in a brace for most of his life. The very same leg. At best it was badly sprained, at worst broken.

Either way, he couldn't walk.

Fighting back tears, Carter called for help. Maybe the elves had survived the Piper's attack. He couldn't have been unconscious for more than a few hours. But he called and called until he was hoarse, and still there was no answer other than his own lonely echoes.

And it was getting dark. His pack and all his supplies had disappeared with the Piper. The landslide had deposited Carter into a gully filled with snow, which had partially broken his fall. He could hear the waves crashing against the shore on the other side of the bluff, and Carter supposed he was lucky he'd fallen down the landward side.

And what had become of the Piper? Carter's final memory before blacking out was of the Piper's alarmed expression as his magic went wild and the cliff face exploded around them both. Had he fallen into the ocean, or been smashed into the rocks below? Either one would be fine with Carter.

But he instantly regretted the thought. The Piper had lost control of his own magic, but he hadn't been trying to hurt Carter, only to get him out of the way.

Regardless, Carter had quite a problem to deal with in the here and now. It was obvious that help wasn't coming, and if Carter was still in that ditch come nightfall, he'd freeze to death. Tentatively, he explored his wounded leg. Though just touching it made him wince, he found the source of the pain right above the ankle. Gently lifting his pants leg, he was relieved to see that the skin wasn't broken. The blood on his clothes was from a dozen different scrapes, but none of them serious. He had a goose-egg bump on his forehead, but at least he hadn't cracked his skull.

That was the good news, but there was almost too much bad news to list. The sun was going down, it was getting colder, and Carter couldn't even stand. A wolf howled in the distance, but not distant enough. The Piper had warned him that timber wolves hunted the borders of the Deep Forest, which was one of the several reasons they'd stuck to the bluffs near the sea.

Carter could manage to pull himself around in a kind of half crawl without putting weight on his injured ankle, but when he tried to climb out of the ditch, he kept sliding. The snow might have helped to cushion his landing, but it made climbing exceedingly difficult. On his second try, a handful of earth and snow came loose in his fingers and he slipped. Reflexively, he stuck out his legs to arrest his fall and landed on his hurt ankle.

With a cry he tumbled back down the gully slope. This time, he did get sick, all down the front of his shirt. For long minutes after that, the best he could do was lie there and breathe until the pain subsided.

Tears welled up in his eyes. He wanted his mother. He wanted his father. He wanted Max. But he was alone in a strange land. No one to pick him up this time—he'd have to do it on his own because if he didn't, he'd die.

He needed to get out of that ditch. And then manage somehow to survive out here in the wild. He prayed that his ankle was sprained and not broken, but even so there would be no walking on it for days, and Carter wouldn't last that long. The Piper had said that the isle healed all wounds in time, but how much time? What other choice did Carter have?

The magic.

The Piper had warned him about the dangers of trying healing magic on himself. For a magician to channel that much magic directly into himself was risky. But maybe, if Carter focused, he could heal himself now.

Or maybe he'd turn his foot into a cherry pie. Still, whatever the risks, Carter had to try. Grudgingly, he thought back to the lessons the Piper had taught him. Magic weighted the odds toward the impossible, and all it usually took was a nudge in the right direction. Carter closed his eyes and pictured the swelling decreasing. He pictured the foot righting itself. Instead of the purple-and-yellow bruise, he visualized healthy pink flesh. As he did so, he searched for the magic, always there, always waiting for him just out of sight. In the past, his need had called the magic, and he needed it more than ever right then.

His scalp began to tingle. Then the tips of his fingers. He reached down and let his fingers play over his hurt ankle, exploring, caressing. The tingle passed into his foot, up to his throbbing ankle. At once the pain diminished—which he took to be a very good sign. But he needed to do more than just deaden the pain; he needed to heal himself. He needed . . .

All at once the pain in his ankle flared red hot, as if it were about to burst into flame. He yelped and tried shutting the magic off, like a spigot. For an instant, he felt enormous pressure all around him, as if a gigantic wave of power were threatening to burst through. It was too much, and he knew that if he let it, it would hurt him. Maybe even kill him.

Carter managed, just barely, to hold the spigot closed, to force the magic away, and gradually the pressure lessened.

Then it was gone.

Carter fell back, exhausted. He felt as if he'd run a marathon, or at least what he imagined it felt like to have run a marathon. His ankle, which had been swollen before, was twice the size now. The throbbing only got worse.

"Whatcha doing?"

A voice, right next to Carter's ear, made him start. He turned to find a small, furry face peering back at him, attached to a potato-shaped body.

"Bandybulb!"

The little kobold nodded, as if his being there in that snowy ditch were the most expected, natural thing in the world. Carter, on the other hand, wanted to grab the little creature in a hug. Quite a change from his usual impulse to toss the kobold far, far away.

"So?" said Bandybulb, blinking at Carter expectantly.

"So . . . what? What do you mean?"

"So what are we doing here in this ditch?" The kobold rubbed his hands together. "It's not the warmest ditch. I've been in warmer by far."

Carter shook his head. "Bandybulb, what are *you* doing here?"

"I saw you lying in a ditch and decided to join you." The kobold leaned forward and whispered. "Are we doing magic? Is this a magic ditch?"

"N-n-no," Carter sputtered. The urge to hug the little

kobold was dissipating. It was quickly being replaced with the other, more familiar urge. It was amazing how the kobold accomplished that. "I mean, how did you get here? How did you find me?"

"Oh, well. I was following the elves on their journey to find you when rocks came tumbling down all around us."

"You were with the elves? Did you see Leetha?"

Bandybulb shook his head. "I have not seen her for some time. After you escaped the elves in the Deep Forest, I decided to follow them because they seemed to know where they were going. I hoped they would lead me to you, and they did!"

"The ones who were caught in the landslide? Did they escape, or are they—"

"Dead? I think not. Elves are very quick and good at dodging falling rocks, I'd imagine."

If Bandybulb was right, then it was a relief. It meant his fight with the Piper meant something.

The kobold put a chubby hand over his heart. "I have traveled all this way to offer you my services because I know that you have a plan to defeat the Piper and save the Summer Isle from winter and darkness." Bandybulb then leaned forward, conspiratorially, and whispered, "So, is this ditch a part of your plan?"

Carter lay back down and laughed. He couldn't help it.

Bandybulb laughed along with him, though it was clear by the look on the kobold's face that he didn't know why. "Whatever it is we are laughing about is hilarious!" said the kobold. "Stop, my cheeks hurt!"

And Carter did stop, because at that moment a wolf's

howl rose again from out of the darkness. This one sounded closer than before. Much closer. It was full night now, and the Winter's Moon was appearing over the trees. If the wolves didn't get them, the dropping temperature would.

"Bandybulb, we have to get out of this ditch."

"Oh, good," said the kobold, clearly relieved. "This is not a very comfortable place. Where should we go?"

Carter pulled himself back to sitting. "I don't know, Bandybulb, I really don't. I'm sorry."

The little kobold sat thoughtfully for a moment. "You are tired and you are hurt. Let me do the thinking for both of us. I will get us out of this ditch. It will all be okay, you'll see."

"I'm sorry I'm disappointing you, Bandybulb."

But Bandybulb stood up and shook his head. "You are not! I came to find you because you never disappoint me, Carter. Because, while not being much brighter than a potato, I know one absolute truth."

"What's that?"

With a chubby little hand on Carter's shoulder, the kobold looked him in the eye. "I know that you would do the same for me."

Carter nodded, because his throat was suddenly too tight with emotion to speak.

"Now," said Bandybulb. "Let's begin by searching this ditch very carefully. I think we are hoping to find a ladder."

Despite the cold, and the not-so-distant howling of wolves, Carter found a familiar smile.

It was going to be a long night.

CHAPTER NINE

awn's arrival in Shades Harbor was more a lightening of the dark than a true sunrise. Far from brightening Lukas's mood, the weak sunlight struggling to penetrate the heavy fog only served to depress him more. Judging by the faces of his companions, he guessed they were feeling much the same. The time spent with the Peddler hadn't been a joyous reunion, but a night of whispered fears and solemn talk of long odds. Foolhardy quests.

But what else was there to do at the start of the new day other than put on your boots and try again? The long odds had never stopped Paul, and his friends would honor him by defying them in his name. For Paul. For Carter.

Max in particular seemed moody and withdrawn. She had slept little, and more than once Lukas had caught her staring into her backpack at the precious contents within.

The only one of his friends who hadn't passed a miserable night had been Harold the trollson. He'd found in the Peddler a receptive, even interested listener to tales of the long, laboriously detailed family tree he was so proud of.

"Now, Helga Stonemuncher, who was quite a catch if the family rumors are to be believed, was really a more metropolitan giant's daughter—that's what we call our females."

The Peddler nodded enthusiastically. "Smart name!"

"Well, she loved the city life, but of course it was hard to find the latest Parisian fashions in giant sizes, so that's when her husband, Bjorn Stonemuncher, decided, with very trollish logic, that the best way to provide pretty dresses roomy enough for his wife to wear would be to kidnap the most famous dressmaker in all of Paris! That led to what my family calls the Great Garment Scandal of 1725."

For Harold, the Peddler was an attentive ear. For the Peddler, Harold was a way to learn about a new generation of magical beings. The trollsons and goblinfolk were the descendants of creatures who'd refused to escape to the Summer Isle those many centuries ago—the ones who'd stayed behind. The elflings, however, were all that was left of the Winter Children, the stolen children of the elves. Around the time the Piper brought the children of Hamelin to the Summer Isle, the elf children went missing—a crime the Piper was also blamed for. As it turned out, the Winter Children ended up on earth, where they grew up, had families, and eventually settled in a dreary place called Bordertown. But some of their descendants, like Max and Carter's housekeeper, Mrs. Amsel, continued to live in secret among the humans.

Max had led those lost peoples—trollsons, goblinfolk and elflings—through Bordertown's last magical door between worlds to this land where they wouldn't have to hide anymore, where summer lasted forever.

Only now summer was over, and maybe for good.

With the sunrise, the rest of the shades disappeared into the mist, but Lukas could still hear their whispers when it was quiet. He could feel their eyes on him.

"They are ready to leave the Summer Isle, but the black boats cannot leave port," explained the Peddler as he walked them to the edge of town.

"Because of the ice?"

The Peddler nodded. "All part of Grannie Yaga's plan, I suspect."

"What good would that do?" asked Max. "What does she care whether ghosts come and go from Shades Harbor?"

"You've seen a gray man, yes? Up close?"

Max paled visibly, and nodded. Lukas himself remembered the creature that had appeared in the darkness of the Piper's prison—a spirit made of rotted flesh and tattered rags—and how it seemed intent on killing them all for no other reason than it could.

"The gray men are Grannie's deadliest allies, but there have never been many of them. Most were murderers in the flesh, and it's their fear and guilt that keep their spirits from passing on to what comes after. But even the gentlest souls will succumb to spite over time, if surrounded by the living. If they are kept from the light, the darkness will take them instead."

Lukas glanced over his shoulder at the worn-down

houses, the lonely streets of Shades Harbor. Lonely, but not empty. They now knew that the village was packed full of unseen spirits. Hundreds. Growing restless, angry.

"There would be an army of them," he breathed. "An army of gray men."

The Peddler spat on the ground. Or at least he went through the motion. Lukas wasn't sure a ghost could actually spit. "Grannie Yaga wants to twist everything in the Summer Isle, living and dead, to evil."

They stopped at the road north, the very edge of Shades Harbor. "This is as far as I go," said the Peddler.

"I'd hoped you might come with us," said Lukas. "At least a little farther."

But the Peddler shook his head. "The ghosts of Shades Harbor aren't yet so far gone that they won't listen to reason. Someone needs to stay here and reassure them that salvation is on the way."

"Salvation?" asked Max.

"This isle will never be the place it once was, but we can at least keep it from becoming a domain of evil. Thwarting Grannie is key to that."

"Then we keep on as we were," said Lukas. "Max and I will continue on to the Deep Forest, and Emilie and Harold will return to New Hamelin."

Emilie arched an eyebrow at him. "Oh, really? Is that an order from the Eldest Boy, then?"

Lukas blushed. The Eldest Boy of the village had no authority over the Eldest Girl, and Emilie darn well knew it. "There are people there who need leadership. And protection. The rat king is probably planning another attack as we speak!"

The Peddler held up a hand. "Do stop bickering, the two of you! Lukas, you need Emilie and Harold. And Max. You cannot do this alone, so stop acting the fool, boy, will you?"

Emilie snickered.

Then the Peddler turned on her. "And you, no more reckless quests in secret!" Emilie's face paled, but the Peddler's scolding tone softened. "Grieving alone is just as foolish, girl. Support each other. Draw strength from that, because you all will need it."

The Peddler turned to address them all, and his stooped ghost seemed to grow taller.

"War has come to the Summer Isle. Your road east will not be an easy one, I fear."

"Like it's been a cakewalk up until now," said Max.

The Peddler went on. "Ogres, rats, witches. The road ahead may seem impossible, but remember that no matter how strong evil becomes, in the end it always turns upon itself. Alliances born out of greed and fear fray quickly, and you may be able to turn that to your advantage.

"Now then," he said. "Max, can I see what it is you hold so dear in that backpack of yours?"

Max glanced at Lukas, but he shrugged—he hadn't told the Peddler anything about Max's parents, or what had been done to them. But it seemed that in death, as in life, the Peddler had a way of knowing things. It was exasperating.

"Okay," said Max, and carefully she set down her

backpack and drew out the two glass jars. Her parents drifted inside, seemingly asleep.

"Well, I haven't seen this in a long time," said the Peddler softly. "A long time. The *vodyanoi*?"

"He called himself Vodnik, but yeah." Max held the jars gently up to the light. "He took my parents and put their souls in these jars to blackmail me into helping him."

The Peddler bent over for a closer look. "Vodnik was always a monster, and I had hoped that the modern world had swallowed him up. Or that he was holed away in some muddy riverbank, unable to harm anyone. I'm sorry."

"Well, he won't be hurting anyone else," said Harold. "He was stepped on by a very large, very rocky trollson."

The Peddler glanced up. "Well, that's both a relief and a shame. Vodnik's magic is sound, meaning that your parents are perfectly safe as long as they are in there. But it also means that if he's dead, it'll take another powerful magician to safely free them." Max looked up at him hopefully, but the Peddler shook his head. "When I was still alive, perhaps. But as a ghost I have no magic to speak of." The old magician smiled. "Have faith, Max. I cannot help them, but if you are in the need of a magician, you have come to the right isle! You will find the magic you need, perhaps in the most unexpected of places."

At that moment, somewhere in the distance, a rooster crowed.

"Ah," said the Peddler. "My time is nearly up, and you all must be about your business. The road ahead is still long, and you'll pass many dangers between here and there. Beware the Bonewood. The evil of that forest has spread well beyond its old borders. Take my old road as far as you can. There may be a little magic left in it that could help you. At the very least you won't get lost!"

Lukas's heart was suddenly full. He stepped forward and extended his hand. "Will we ever see you again, Peddler?"

The old ghost—for now in the morning light he looked more ghost than man—stared at Lukas's hand for a moment before closing his own around it. Lukas couldn't feel flesh, nothing solid, just a cold mist tingling his fingertips.

"I think not," said the Peddler. "But I'm glad that your path brought you this way. We've earned a proper goodbye."

Emilie wiped her eyes and said, "Peddler, if you should ever see Paul, in this world or the next . . . tell him I miss him."

"I will. But I promise you, he already knows."

The rooster crowed again, and the Peddler was gone.

CHAPTER TEN

Carter and Bandybulb built their campfire up high, until it was a blazing bonfire, because the fire was the only thing keeping the wolves at bay. The pair had passed a sleepless night, flinching at shadows in the dark. From just beyond the light of the fire they could hear low growls and the padding of soft feet in the snow.

And the wolves' eyes gleamed red when they dared enter the firelight. Carter remembered Lukas telling him once that in the early days, fire had been the only weapon the children of Hamelin had. The beasts of the wild, even the clever rats, all shared an instinctual fear of it. Whether that beast was hungry enough, or mean enough, to overcome that fear, well, that was most likely the difference between living and dying. Carter desperately hoped that the wolves had eaten recently and that they could wait a day or two more and not risk getting burned for such a light snack as Carter and Bandybulb would make.

Thankfully, one by one the wolves abandoned the hunt. They'd moved on to search for easier prey. Only one wolf remained as the sun came up, but unfortunately it was a big one. A massive wolf, the size of a pony, with sleek, silver fur, and paws and muzzle as black as last night's cloudless sky. It watched patiently as Carter and Bandybulb's fire gradually died down. The firewood was nearly spent, and although Carter could conjure fire, he couldn't sustain it for very long. Without wood for fuel, their campfire would soon go out.

Which, as unlikely as it sounded, seemed to be what the wolf was waiting for. As the morning wore on, the wolf just sat there. Every now and again it would lick its paw or scratch. That's it.

"Perhaps the wolf would go away if you used your magic to set *it* on fire?" Bandybulb suggested.

Carter propped himself up on the crooked branch he'd been using as a crutch. He'd used strips of cloth from his cloak to wrap his ankle, and packed the makeshift bandages with snow. The swelling seemed to have reduced slightly, and Carter hoped against hope that it was just a bad sprain. "I don't want to use magic against the wolf unless we have no other choice. The way my magic's been working, I'd say there was a fifty-fifty chance I'd set *us* on fire by mistake."

Bandybulb sighed as he warmed his butt near the meager remains of their campfire. "Well then, I suppose I will have to prepare myself for becoming breakfast instead of eating it."

"There has to be another way," said Carter. "Maybe we can scare it off with rocks or something. I mean, it's not even pacing or anything—it's just sitting there!" Carter inched closer, careful not to put any weight on his bad foot. "Shoo! Get! Get out of here, you stupid mutt! Go on!"

"Yeah!" cried Bandybulb. "Go scratch your fleas somewhere else and please don't eat us, okay?"

"Hmm," answered the wolf. "I'll think about it."

Carter and Bandybulb exchanged a look of surprise. And alarm.

"Uh-oh," said Bandybulb. "I don't think you should have called him stupid."

The wolf let out something between a bark and a human-sounding laugh. "'Him'? I am a she-wolf, kobold, so watch your tongue."

Bandybulb threw up his hands. "Easy mistake! He . . . er, *she* doesn't sound like a she-wolf, does she, Carter?"

"I wouldn't know," said Carter. "I've never heard a wolf talk before." He cleared his throat. "Uh, so, Ms. Wolf, you can talk, which shouldn't really surprise me here on the Summer Isle, I guess. But what do you want?"

The wolf cocked her head at him. "Don't worry, I've already eaten. I heard those simple wolves carrying on last night and came here to see what all the fuss was about. A kobold and a human boy? I must admit I'm disappointed."

Bandybulb jabbed a finger in the wolf's direction. "You'd best beware! Carter here is a master magician."

"So you say," answered the wolf. "But he doesn't smell all that dangerous. He smells wounded and afraid."

"I'm not a master magician," said Carter. He didn't think empty boasting would go very far with this creature, since she could apparently smell the truth beneath the lies. "But I do know a little magic, and I can protect us if I need to. I'd just rather not hurt anyone."

The wolf rose and trotted a few steps closer, and Carter immediately retreated, nearly tripping over Bandybulb and into the fire.

"Ouch!" cried the little kobold.

"Sorry."

The wolf let out a low growl. "You human cubs and your fires. You are so careless, I'm amazed you haven't all burned down your own village in your sleep."

"Village? You've been to New Hamelin?"

"I've seen it, and the children who live there. But you don't smell like them."

"No," answered Carter. "I'm . . . a visitor. From somewhere far away."

"Recently come to the Summer Isle?" the wolf asked.

"I guess."

"You wouldn't have anything to do with this winter, would you?" At this, the wolf's hackles began to rise.

"No, no!" said Carter quickly. "The winter is Grannie Yaga's fault. She murdered the Peddler, and that's when the summer started to turn to winter."

This answer, which also happened conveniently to be the truth, seemed to satisfy the wolf. "The Peddler's death is a great loss to us all."

"He was your friend?" asked Carter.

"There were times when we were friendly, times when we were not. But the Peddler was kind to all animals on the Summer Isle."

"I never met him," said Carter. "But I wish I could have."

"And what about you?" asked the wolf. "What brings you to the edge of this isle, so far from home? You are near the elves' domain, you know, and they don't look kindly upon strangers."

Carter wasn't sure how much to say. How far should he trust a strange talking wolf who'd appeared out of nowhere?

"I was traveling with someone, but we got separated. Now I'm a bit lost."

"This someone was a friend of yours?"

"No. I mean, not exactly. We were just traveling together because we were headed for the same place."

"Where's that?"

Carter hesitated. If the Piper was still alive, he'd be headed to Magician's Landing. That meant that if Carter was still going to stop him, he needed to get there first. But being hobbled, he wasn't sure he could find it without the Piper's help. He could try and climb the cliffs again to navigate by sight, but that would be nearly impossible with his leg the way it was. Perhaps this wolf could help.

Carter couldn't see any better options. "We're trying to find Magician's Landing. Do you know the way?"

The wolf squatted and nipped at something itching her flank. "Now, why would a human boy and a kobold want to go to a place like that? It's just an old ruin. If you'd like, I could show you the Deep Forest. Wonders there to behold. Plentiful game for hunting."

"And elves for hanging you up by your toes," warned Bandybulb.

"You'll be safe with me," said the wolf, but Bandybulb emphatically shook his head.

"Thanks for the kind offer," said Carter. "But we're going to Magician's Landing. Could you at least point us in the right direction?"

The wolf's ears perked up as she sniffed the wind. "A storm is coming, and it will bring even more snow. The way would not be easy for you even if you weren't lame."

Carter gritted his teeth at the word. "I'm not lame. I can make it—I just need to know the way." He shifted his weight, as the makeshift crutch was already biting into his armpit. He could barely manage walking with it now; it was harder still to imagine doing so in a few feet of snow. But what other choice did he have? "Please," he added.

The she-wolf sniffed the air again and ran her tongue over her finger-long canines. "Tastes like change on the wind. Danger. But I'm curious about you, still." Then the wolf looked up at the seaside cliffs. "Follow me. I will lead you to Magician's Landing by a path only wolves know."

"Thank you," said Carter. "What should we call you?"

"Blackpaw."

"I'm Carter. This is Bandybulb."

The kobold waved. "Pleased to meet you."

Wordlessly, Blackpaw turned and trotted off.

Bandybulb tugged on Carter's pants leg. "I do not think this is a good idea. I had an uncle who was once eaten by a wolf, and he never spoke highly of the experience."

"You mean he was once bitten, not eaten."

The kobold looked up at him and blinked, not grasping the important distinction.

"Look," said Carter. "I need to get to Magician's Landing. I'm taking my chances." Leaning on the crutch, he started after the wolf, one painful step after another.

Bandybulb sighed, but he followed along. "Fine, but don't complain to me after you get eaten. Uncle Spoutsnout never stopped going on about it."

PART II

THE MARCH TO WAR

CHAPTER ELEVEN

K ing Wormling hated winter. True, the long nights
suited him well, and if the rat never saw the sun
again, that would be just fine. But Wormling was
not a young rat, and the snow clumped in his fur, and the
cold made his joints ache. Worst of all, rough weather made
foraging and raiding even harder than usual for his subjects,
and hungry bellies led to rebellious thoughts.

The unchanging winter might very well mean that evil
was nearly triumphant on the Summer Isle, that good was
on the run. Grannie Yaga might be right about all of that,
but Wormling couldn't give two knucklebones about good
and evil. This war of hers was already bringing unexpected
troubles. It had been the witch's idea to attack New Hamelin when they did, long before Wormling thought them
ready. Why only four ogres? Why not raise a proper army of
the brutes? What was the hurry?

The siege had failed, as had every one before it. Serious damage had been done to Wormling's credibility as king, since the rat ruled not by physical strength but by cunning— and results. He'd promised the rat kingdom victories, and if he didn't keep that promise he'd end up with his tail chewed off and his throne robbed from under him.

There was always another rat waiting to steal your dinner.

And now to summon Wormling halfway across the isle, back to this rats-forsaken place, through the mountains and across the Great River into the Dark Moors, to the Black Tower itself . . . the witch had some nerve. Too bad she was dangerous enough to have earned it.

Wormling rubbed his newly fat belly and rummaged around in his filthy palanquin for a duck's egg. He wasn't hungry, but stuffing oneself to near bursting was a perk that came along with the throne. Wormling the spy, Wormling the sneak had been a scrawny, pitiful creature. Wormling the king would be fat, fat, fat.

As he bit through the brittle shell, the palanquin jostled and the delicious yolk ran all down Wormling's chin. Furious, he stuck his head out the covered window. One of the human slaves carrying the king had stumbled and fallen. The child was struggling to get back to his feet, but the ground was slick with snow and ice. One of the rat slave-drivers was stalking toward the child, whip in hand.

"Get on your feet, runt," the slave driver snarled. "I'll whip you raw!"

"Hold your lash," commanded Wormling. These petty, small-brained rats were always too quick to become violent.

Never used their wits at all. "If you whip the child now, how well will he carry my palanquin the rest of the way?"

The slave driver held his whip in quivering hands. Reluctantly, he lowered it. "Yes, my king."

"Help the child to his feet."

Fur bristling in shame, the slave driver took the child's arm and yanked him to standing. The child glanced up at Wormling, his normally haggard, tired eyes brimming with thankfulness.

"What's your name, child?"

"M-Marc, sire."

"Good. Driver, you can whip Marc when we reach our destination," called Wormling. "And an extra lash for looking his king in the eyes." Then he settled back into his seat and sucked on another egg.

❖

The Black Tower itself was unchanged since the last time Wormling had seen it. A spindly, crooked spire amidst a pile of long-forgotten ruins, it had been used for centuries as the Piper's prison. The last time Wormling had been here, he'd been serving King Marrow. This time Wormling paused outside the tower only briefly, remembering the spot where the old rat king had taken an elf girl's knife in the back. Wormling had been hiding nearby, and he'd seen the knife coming for his king. He could have called out a warning, given Marrow the opportunity to defend himself. He could've, but he hadn't. And now Marrow was dead and Wormling was king. Life was funny that way.

As Wormling passed through the doorway, he made sure to look over his shoulder.

At the top of the tower's twisting stairs, he found a single chamber with a warm peat fire roaring inside the hearth and a cold cauldron in the corner. Wormling gratefully took his place by the fire as he nodded to the room's sole occupant.

Org, newly crowned chieftain of the Bonewood ogres, blinked his beady eyes at Wormling and grunted. There was a time not too long ago when Org had stood by Wormling's side, a bodyguard generously provided by the witch. It seemed that Org had moved up in the world. Grannie, of course, would be to blame.

As Wormling warmed his backside near the fire, he realized he'd been wrong about Org being the only other creature in the room. Standing in the shadows—no, a *part* of the shadows—and far from the firelight was a figure wrapped all in tattered rags. A gray man. So Grannie was joining with far more dangerous allies than rats and ogres. The gray men were hateful spirits, and it was well known that they despised all living things. Just looking at it seemed to suck the warmth from Wormling's plump body. Even Org was keeping his distance. It was said that the gray men could not abide fire, however. Wormling scooted even closer to the flames.

"Have you been waiting long, Org?" Wormling asked. The ogre grunted something that might have been a yes. Might have been gas, it was hard to tell with ogres. In any case, small talk was over.

Luckily, it wasn't long before Wormling heard the sound of flapping wings outside the chamber window. He barely had time to turn his head before Grannie Yaga was standing before them.

Was it Wormling's imagination, or was the old witch looking more stooped than usual? The last time he'd seen her, she hadn't needed a walking stick, but tonight she leaned heavily on a gnarled ropewood cane. As she hobbled into the firelight, Wormling almost let out a gasp—she had a scabbed-over wound where one eye should be.

Seeing his reaction, the witch smiled at him, showing her ugly wooden teeth. "I was pretty before, but I thinks I'm even prettier now, eh? It'll heal with time, don't you worry."

She cackled as Wormling looked away. "Let's get this over with," he said.

Grannie waved a hand over the cauldron in the corner, sprinkling powder of some kind into it. At once, whatever liquid was inside began to glow green, and bubble. Then the green light faded and Wormling could see a reflection in the cauldron, but not of Grannie. The image floating along the surface was that of a darkened cave opening. Something large, white and fleshy was moving around in there.

"Roga, dear," Grannie cooed. "The council meeting's starting."

Whatever that enormous thing was inside that dark hole, it came close enough that Wormling could see a pair of yellowish eyes peering out.

"Sister," said a throaty voice. "You are not looking good. That's nice to see."

"A shame you've grown too fat to leave your cave, or else you could taunt me in person."

Grannie smiled, but her one good eye was full of hate.

"Now that we've all met," continued the witch, "time for talking."

"Wait," said Wormling. "Aren't we missing one? Where's your precious Piper?"

Grannie's face darkened. "Where indeed? Sister?"

Wormling could hear Roga shifting around, even through the cauldron window. Her massive weight scraped against rock and stone. Wormling patted his own round belly. Perhaps he should lay off the eggs.

"Roga sees all," said Grannie. "But she cannot see our dear lost Piper, ain't that right?"

"He's hidden himself from me. Or is being hidden, I cannot say."

"It matters not," said Grannie. "We don't need the Piper to talk about what needs doing."

"And what's that?" asked Wormling. "I've come a long way on short notice."

"War, good king rat." The witch tapped her cane on the stone floor. "This is a war council, after all."

Wormling thought of the debacle that had been the siege of New Hamelin, of the pathetic number of rat warriors who'd come back from that battle, licked and limping. He thought of more lying dead outside the Hameliners' sturdy wooden gates, and what he wanted to say to Grannie Yaga was that she could take her war and choke on it. Wormling, the rat king, would tear down the walls of New Hamelin in his own time, in his own way. He'd see the children all wearing chains of their own making, and he'd do it without the witch's help.

But Wormling didn't say any of that. He glanced instead at the gray man lurking in the shadows, and back to Grannie. "How might the rat army help you in this war, Grannie Yaga?"

"Good boy." Yaga patted Wormling's head, and he resisted the urge to bite her finger off. "You make your Grannie proud."

"Forgive my ignorance, but the Peddler's dead," said Wormling. "The Princess hasn't dared to show herself in ages. New Hamelin won't stand for much longer. After that, who's left to fight?"

"The boy Carter," said Grannie. The witch strode to the center of the chamber and took them all in with her one good eye. "Evil is winning—yes, we are—but that's not the same as having won. You all know my gift. Just as sure as my sister has the gift of seeing the present, Grannie Yaga sees what is yet to come, and I seen the last son of Hamelin freeing the Piper from his prison, which Carter has. But now the boy's usefulness is finished."

A low moan of hunger came from Roga, drifting out through the cauldron, and Wormling actually felt his stomach turn. He had no love for the children of Hamelin, but the diet of witches was nothing he liked to think about. Far better to put the children to work, as the rats did. To teach them who their proper masters were.

He made a mental note to keep an eye on his own slaves around Grannie. As prisoners of war, they were hard to come by. And there was something in the witch's voice when she spoke of the boy Carter, something Wormling had recognized in her before. Fear. After a lifetime spent cowering, Wormling could smell fear on others. He smelled it on Grannie whenever she spoke of the boy. Carter, for whatever reason, frightened her.

"While I certainly wouldn't want to deprive you of your treats, Grannie," said Wormling, "have you considered that the Piper and Carter may be together? If both of them are missing, then might they be allies?"

Grannie scoffed at this, but Wormling could smell the worry on her. "I spent centuries pouring poison into the Piper's ears. He's one of us, with a heart as black as pitch."

A low rumble came from Org. Not even the ogre, thick as he was, believed Grannie on this. It was far too great a coincidence.

"So what do we do?" asked Wormling. "Where do we look for the boy?"

"Leave that to me. In the meantime, you all prepare your forces and wait for my call."

Org grunted and the gray man stayed ever silent, which Wormling assumed was his way of agreeing. If he wanted to disagree, he'd probably just kill you and be done with it. Only Wormling seemed to have misgivings about possibly going to war over a single human child.

Still, he knew better than to openly question the witch any more than he already had. Wormling was patient, especially when he smelled weakness. And Grannie reeked of it. There was something here she wasn't saying. Something that despite her centuries of planning had gone dangerously awry. The Piper and Carter were at the center of it, and

Wormling would bide his time until he figured out a way to turn it to his advantage.

In the meantime, he would kiss the witch's ugly behind. "The rat kingdom as always is at your command, Grannie." He bowed low enough to lick the stone floor. "Point us in the direction of your enemies and we will fight for you; only allow me to lead the charge when the time comes!"

Grannie chuckled. "Well, Wormling, is that a spine growing inside all that new girth? Very well, rat king. The lead is yours. Org's ogres will support you and the gray men will . . . do as they do."

And when all is said and done, thought Wormling, *when the rat kingdom stretches from one coast of the Summer Isle to the other—then there will be no room for witches!*

CHAPTER TWELVE

"I wish we could've eaten breakfast before we left." Harold's stomach let out a loud, gurgling rumble. "See what I mean? Sorry."

"That's all right," answered Lukas. His own empty belly gnawed at him, but when a trollson's stomach growled, it was noisy enough to wake the living and the dead. Well, hopefully not the dead. Lukas had already seen his fill of ghosts.

In what might have been a sign of worse weather to come, a gentle snow had begun to fall. Lukas encouraged the rest to pick up their pace just to be safe. He wanted to cover as many miles as possible before nightfall, even if that meant not stopping for meals. To reach the Deep Forest they had to first pass through the Bonewood, the wicked forest that took its name from the skeletal trees that grew there.

It was a dangerous place. The last time Lukas and his friends had walked this road, the Bonewood was still fenced in by the Peddler's magic. But now with the Peddler dead, there was nothing to keep that evil forest in check. The Bonewood was growing.

They hadn't gone more than a few miles before it came into view, and what a view it was. Leafless trees, with bark the color of parchment or bone, and twisting boughs and grasping branches to bar your way. The Peddler's Road had once marked the Bonewood's border, but now it curved through what looked more like the heart of the wood, so dense were the trees on either side. The forest had spread that far, that fast.

"So that's why they call it the Bonewood, huh?" said Harold. "Looks like a bunch of giant, bony fingers growing out of the dirt."

"How it looks is the least of our problems," said Emilie. "Ogres roam these woods, and nixies and nokks swim in ponds waiting for unwary travelers."

Lukas blanched. The last time they'd traveled this way, he'd very nearly been drowned by a nokk, an evil water creature that had pulled him to the bottom of a fouled creek. Max had saved him then, but Lukas had no desire to put her to the test again. "We'll stay clear of any streams or ponds, agreed?"

"No argument here," said Max. "But the sooner we go in, the sooner we can make it out the other side, right?"

Lukas nodded. "Let's make sure we stay together in there. Max and I in the lead, Emilie and Harold right behind." He drew his sword. "Just in case."

"Yeah, just in case," said Max.

The four of them picked their path carefully among the

broken bricks that marked what had once been the Peddler's Road. The creeping vines and tree roots had done their best to erase all traces of the road, but there was still enough of a path to follow. The Bonewood hadn't been able to swallow it whole, and not even the freshly fallen snow could hide it completely. Lukas remembered what the Peddler had said about there being a little magic left in it. Maybe it would be enough to keep them safe until they reached the other side of the forest.

Maybe.

The forest was bare of undergrowth except for the thorny vines that threatened to trip the heedless traveler, and the grave moss growing along the tree trunks, across the stones at their feet. It was quiet like no other forest. No birds sang. No squirrels skittered along the branches. There was no sound other than the crunch of their boots on the snowy ground, and even that seemed too loud to Lukas's ears. It felt like stomping in a church—or more precisely, a graveyard.

They hiked along the ruined road for an hour, which turned into two, and still no end was in sight. In all that time they saw not a single animal. But that didn't mean they were alone in the Bonewood. They all could feel eyes watching them. A prickle at the back of Lukas's neck told him that something was tracking every step he took. It had started out as a feeling of wariness, but the deeper they went into the forest, the angrier it got—whatever *it* was, the trees themselves maybe. All Lukas knew was that something did not want them there, and the longer they stayed, the more certain he grew that they were in danger.

It wasn't until late in the day that a threat revealed itself.

They rounded a bend in the road and found themselves face to face with an ogre.

It was not, however, the sort of ogre Lukas was used to. The tree-trunk legs, round belly and beady eyes were to be expected, but this ogre did not travel alone. A small, sour-faced creature rode upon his back, perched inside some kind of open wooden basket. But strangest of all, the little creature was holding leather reins in both hands that attached to a harness around the ogre's thick neck.

"Goblin!" breathed Emilie, next to Lukas. "I think that's a goblin . . . riding an ogre?"

The goblin's sizable ears picked up Emilie's words. "Not any goblin, child. Me name's Pricklestick, warlord of the Bonewood! You be trespassing on my land, and now you must pay the toll."

The goblin produced a sack, twice as big as he was, and tossed it onto the ground at their feet. Then he whipped the reins, and the ogre dutifully stepped forward. "Valuables in the sack," the goblin sneered. "Pay up, or die!"

There was a tense moment of silence as the friends looked at each other. "We don't want to fight if we don't have to," whispered Emilie. Lukas agreed, but they weren't exactly carrying any valuables.

Harold cleared his throat. "Um, I've got a pack of gum. Will that do?"

The goblin, Pricklestick, squinted at Harold. "Eh? What be *gum,* then?"

Lukas was wondering the same thing.

"It's kind of a treat," said Harold. "From where I come from. Right, Max?"

Max looked uncertain. "Uh, sure."

"Here, watch." Harold took a small sliver of something out of the packet and popped it into his mouth. He chewed it and kept on chewing. "See? Gum."

The goblin's eyes lit up as he barked in the ogre's ear. "Gud, fetch me yonder gum!"

The ogre reached out a meaty paw and took the package from Harold. He sniffed it and seemed to like what he smelled, but Pricklestick snatched it away from the ogre's maw.

"Mine!" he cried. The goblin unwrapped the package and, after examining a piece of gum up close, he put it tentatively in his mouth.

"M-hmm, 'tis good."

"That's it," said Harold. "Just keep chewing it."

Pricklestick did as he was told. Lukas looked at the two in confusion. Seconds went by and they both were still chewing those tiny slivers.

"Don't swallow it," said Harold.

"No?" said Pricklestick.

"Nope."

"How about now? Can I swallow it now?"

"Nuh-uh." Harold kept contentedly chewing.

The goblin took a few more pieces and stuffed them into his mouth.

"When *can* I swallow?" he asked, his words barely comprehensible through his full mouth.

"Well, never."

"What?" Pricklestick spat a ball of well-chewed glop

into his palm. "What sort of cursed food is it that can never be eaten? 'Tis torture!"

Harold scratched his head. "Well, you weren't supposed to put it all in your mouth at once. . . ."

"Uh-oh," said Max.

"Gud!" cried Pricklestick in a rage. "Smash them!"

With a bellow, the ogre charged. Lukas turned to shove Max out of the way, only to find that the girl had already dodged clear. Suddenly it was Lukas who needed saving as the ogre came at him, ham-sized fists swinging.

Lukas may not have had an ogre on a leash, but thankfully he did have a friend who happened to be a trollson. Harold met Gud's charge with a tackle of his own, and the two giants toppled to the ground with a clamorous thud. Pricklestick, tossed from his basket, went flying.

The goblin stood up on wobbly legs, and seeing Harold and Gud rather evenly matched and wrestling on the ground, he started to make his escape.

"Max!" shouted Lukas. "Stop him!"

But it was Emilie who was closest to the fleeing goblin, and as he ran past she stuck out one leg, tripping him. Pricklestick landed face-first in the dirt.

"Arg, me nose!" he cried, but not before Emilie managed to snatch Pricklestick's extra-large sack up off the ground and toss it over the goblin. The little creature cried out a string of terrible curses as she cinched up the sack tight around him.

"Like catching a weasel in a flour sack," she said as she lifted the squirming bundle with both hands.

"Good work, Emilie," said Lukas. Then he leaned down and shouted into the sack. "Pricklestick, call off your ogre."

"Go stuff yer head in a hole!" replied the muffled voice within.

Lukas took his sword and gently poked the trapped goblin. Not hard enough to hurt, but enough for him to understand the situation. "Call him off, goblin. Now."

There were some whispered expletives that either Lukas had never heard before or were just then made up by the goblin. Then Pricklestick shouted, "Gud, heel, boy. That's a good ogre, now."

Harold and Gud stopped their fighting almost immediately. The two were frozen for a moment on the ground, wrapped in hand-to-hand combat. Slowly, Gud released a handful of Harold's hair and Harold took his fingers out of Gud's nose.

"You let me out now?" asked Pricklestick. "'Tis stuffy in here, 'tis!"

Emilie looked at Lukas. "What do you think? I say no."

"Aw! Gud didn't kill you!" said Pricklestick. "Why be you so mad?"

"Quiet, you." Emilie gave the sack a rough shake. Pricklestick squealed and went silent. "Goblins," she sighed.

Lukas eyed the ogre warily, but apparently Gud was perfectly happy not to smash people when he wasn't being ordered to. At the moment, he was contentedly digging dirt out of his navel. "*If* we decide to let him go, I want to know a few things first."

"Humiliating, 'tis," whined the goblin in the sack. "Shameful."

"How much farther until we reach the end of the Bonewood?"

"Keep walking and you will reach the end before day turns to night, you will."

Lukas studied the patches of sky visible above the trees. It was hard to tell in an overcast sky, but he guessed they had only a few hours of daylight left. Five hours of forest left ahead of them. And the snow was picking up. Branches groaned in the wind. A storm was definitely on its way. If the storm slowed them down, they wouldn't make it out before nightfall.

"Is there anyplace to take shelter on the road ahead?" Lukas asked. "Someplace safe?"

"Yes, yes, there be an ogre mound not an hour's hike yonder. You could shelter there."

"Emilie? Shake him please."

"Wait! Wait!" the goblin cried. "I be telling ye the truth! The Bonewood's near cleared out, 'tis. All ogre mounds is empty, ever since Grannie called them that's loyal to do battle for her."

"What are you talking about? What about Gud here?"

"Gud didn't go on account he's a runt. The other ogres wouldn't have him, so I put him to work."

"You mean you made him your slave," said Emilie.

"No! We be partners, him and me. Truly."

Lukas had to admit, Pricklestick sounded earnest for once. And now that he thought about it, Gud did seem on the smallish side for an ogre, luckily for Harold.

"What does Grannie Yaga want with the ogres?" Lukas asked.

"War. Grannie's big war. She been gathering all the mean beasts of the wood and dark places to fight for her—rats and ogres, and worse, I reckon."

"That doesn't sound good," said Max.

Lukas agreed. He immediately thought of New Hamelin and all the children there, plus the refugees from Bordertown. "Listen, Pricklestick, because this is important. Answer this wrong, try and lie or wriggle your way out of it, and I'll have Emilie toss this sack into the river, understand?"

"Sure, you be clear as a bell."

"You say Grannie's putting together an army. Where are they attacking?"

"Why, 'tis the direction you're heading, 'tis. Grannie's setting siege to the Deep Forest. Thinks the elves are hiding some human boy from her and she wants him. She wants him bad."

Lukas felt Max tense up beside him. They hadn't been fast enough. Grannie knew where Carter was, and she was willing to go to war to get him. "Don't worry," Lukas whispered. "The elves won't give up without a fight. Grannie may have bitten off more than she can chew. We'll get to him in time. I promise."

But secretly, he wondered if that was even possible. New Hamelin had withstood an attack from a joint force of rats and a handful of ogres, but this was every ogre in the Bonewood, with the exception of Gud, it seemed. Who could stand up to a force like that?

CHAPTER THIRTEEN

"Do you think she's gone off and abandoned us?" asked Bandybulb. The little kobold had snuggled up to Carter for warmth, and it was only in being this close that Carter had realized that the kobold didn't just look like an old potato, he kind of smelled like one, too. Weird.

Blackpaw was tireless, and when Carter and the kobold had to stop and rest (which was often), she would leave them to scout ahead. But she had been gone for longer than usual this time—a lot longer. His ankle was grateful not to be moving, and at least the throbbing had stopped, but he stayed warmer on his feet, with his blood pumping.

"I don't know," said Carter. "But if she doesn't come back soon, we're going to have to keep on ourselves. Try and find shelter until this storm passes." He rubbed his already numb fingers. "Do you think any kobolds live around here?"

"Not any sane ones."

"Well, if we try to spend the night out here in the open, we're goners."

"It's a shame your magic isn't working."

"It's not like that." Carter looked into the desperate eyes of his little friend. "I'm too tired to make a simple fire. The Piper asked me once to conjure a pie, but I couldn't even manage that without screwing it up. I'm not a real magician, Bandybulb. Not a good one, anyway."

"That's too bad," sighed Bandybulb. "I could really go for a piece of pie."

At that moment a shape appeared in the storm. "Look, it's Blackpaw."

The great she-wolf approached them slowly, her head low to the ground and teeth bared.

"What's she doing?" asked Bandybulb. "Oh, I was right! She's going to eat us! I hate it when I am right!"

Carter tried to shush him, but Blackpaw still stalked toward them. Carter could hear her growl, a low rumble beneath the blowing wind. "Blackpaw? It's us!"

The wolf crept closer.

Desperately, Carter tried to reach for the magic, but he was exhausted. So sore and so very tired. It was like trying to grab paint spilled in a stream: every grab just made it that much farther away.

With a snarl, Blackpaw lunged. Heroically, stupidly, Bandybulb tried to shield Carter with his round little body. But Blackpaw didn't pounce on them. Instead, she leaped *over* them before dashing off into the storm. The snow was too thick for Carter to see what happened next, but he heard Blackpaw barking furiously and another sound, like a squealing hiss.

Then silence.

Nothing moved except for the wind.

"Blackpaw?" Carter peered into the blowing snow for any sign of the wolf.

She reappeared dragging a dead rat creature by the scruff of its neck. Across its chest the rat wore a leather bandolier stuffed with crude knives.

Blackpaw dropped the rat's corpse on the ground and sat, licking the blood from her lips.

"Whoa," said Bandybulb. For once, he'd captured Carter's thoughts exactly.

"What . . . ?" Carter started. "Where did that come from?"

"I picked up the rat's scent when the wind changed. I circled back around, hoping to surprise it, but the creature was crafty. I would say it's been following your trail for a while now."

"I didn't know there were any rats this far south," said Bandybulb.

"There shouldn't be," answered Blackpaw. "This one was a scout, but the rats never dare stray this close to the Deep Forest." She sniffed the air.

"What do you think it was doing?" asked Carter.

"Hunting you." For a moment Blackpaw looked torn. The she-wolf kept glancing over her shoulder toward the forest, her home, and then back to Carter.

Then, her mind made up, she trotted over to Carter and nudged him with her snout. "Come. Where there is one rat there will be more. We have to assume that the rat king has scouts along the coast looking for you. We must go faster."

Carter stood up, awkwardly, on his crutch. "I'm ready."

"No," said Blackpaw. "Too slow. Here." She lowered her forelegs to the ground. "I will carry both of you."

Carter glanced at Bandybulb. The little kobold was shaking his head and mouthing, *She's going to eat us.*

Blackpaw was certainly big enough to carry them. And Carter was so very tired.

With effort, he managed to swing his leg over the she-wolf's back. Her fur was soft and warm beneath the clumps of crusted snow.

"Come on, Bandybulb. You, too."

Still shaking his head, the little kobold hopped on. "I should let you know, Blackpaw, that kobolds taste like rotten vegetables. Very bitter."

The she-wolf turned her head to look at him. "I know." If a wolf could smile, she was doing it then.

Then Blackpaw was off, loping through the snow and storm, with Carter and Bandybulb barely managing to hang on.

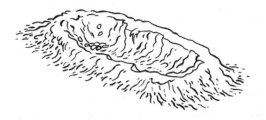

CHAPTER FOURTEEN

With Pricklestick to guide them, Max and her friends did in fact spend the night in ogre mounds—an experience none of them wanted to repeat ever again. An ogre mound was basically just that, a massive mound of dirt with just enough room dug into its middle for an ogre to sleep lying down. Two mounds fit the four of them well enough, with Harold getting his own. Nevertheless, the four friends took turns keeping watch throughout the night and an eye on the goblin and his ogre. The ogres managed to make the insides of their dirt mounds dirtier than the outside, and smelly. But at least the travelers stayed warm and dry as they weathered the snowstorm raging outside.

In the morning, they came to the end of the Bonewood. In between curses and occasional pleas for mercy, the goblin had warned them that Grannie's forces were gathering, but that still didn't prepare Max for what awaited them. The Bonewood had spread almost to the banks of the Eastern Fork, where a long wooden bridge spanned the river. On the far shore, the Deep Forest loomed like a mountain range, and to the north of that, the Dark Moors went on for miles upon miles.

Stretching out along the moors, near the edge of the forest, the largest army any of them had ever seen was gearing up for war. The attack on New Hamelin had been carried out by a mix of rats and a few ogres, but this was a true invasion force. Rats, so many rats. Max was at once reminded of the swarm of rats that had invaded her family's kitchen back in Germany. Hundreds, thousands of them had come spilling out of the wall. They'd been everywhere she'd looked. But this was many times worse. Every rat on the Summer Isle must have answered Grannie's call to battle, and each one was as big as a person.

Worse still were the ogres. Just four of the brutes had nearly torn down the walls of New Hamelin, but there were scores of them gathered here. Leetha the elf girl was probably the best fighter Max had ever seen, and if all elves were as dangerous as she was, the Deep Forest would not be easy to conquer. But even so, Max didn't see how anyone could stand against the horde massing outside their borders.

Harold summed it up perfectly when he leaned down and said, "That's a lot of bad guys."

"Yeah, it's a good thing we don't have to go through them," Max said. "We can sneak downstream until we're out of sight, find a way to cross the river and enter the Deep

Forest there. If we tell the elves we know Leetha, hopefully they'll let us in."

Pricklestick let out a sudden yelp, and Max and Harold looked over to where Emilie and Lukas were huddled around their goblin-in-a-sack prisoner. Gud the ogre, who'd up until now seemed perfectly content to pick his nose, glanced up worriedly at the sound.

Max and Harold quickly hurried over to Emilie and Lukas. "Uh, guys?" Max said. "Whatever you're doing, you'd better cut it out. It's making Gud nervous."

"Yeah, I really don't feel like wrestling him again right now," added Harold.

But Emilie just shook the sack holding Pricklestick even more roughly. "You tell them, goblin! Tell them what you just told us."

"Ah, the mad girl's shaking me brains loose!"

"Tell them!"

"All right, all right! Could you give me a spot of air to breathe at least?"

"Better do it," whispered Max. Gud was looking anxiously their way, one finger in his ear.

"Do it," said Lukas. "But then you need to talk, Pricklestick."

Emilie loosened the sack just enough so that the little goblin could poke his head out, but no more.

"Ah!" he breathed. "You've no idea how bad you stink until you're stuck smelling only yourself all day."

"Tell them," said Emilie.

The goblin sighed. "When Grannie called the ogres

to join her army there, Gud and I marched along with 'em until they kicked the poor wee runt out. And I saw them rats with their children."

Max shook her head, confused. "You mean the rats brought their young to war with them?"

"Not rat children, human children. Like you folk. They was wearing chains and fetching water for the rats, carrying their weapons. Them slow ones got the whip fast enough, too."

"Slaves," said Lukas, mouth tight with anger. "He's talking about the lost children of New Hamelin that were captured by the rats. It looks like they brought them along to war."

Max didn't know what to say. She knew that Lukas and Emilie suspected the rats had been using the captive children as slaves, but none of them were expecting to find them here, of all places.

Lukas looked at her, a battle of emotions plainly visible on his face. "Marc, Leon. While they were being kept inside the rat king's lair, it seemed almost impossible to rescue them, but now . . . Max, we may never have this chance again."

But that means waiting to find Carter. That was what he was really trying to say. If the lost children of New Hamelin were being kept as slaves down there in that war camp, and if Lukas, Max and their companions dared to try a rescue, it would mean delaying their search for her brother. And that was if they survived such a dangerous attempt at all. Max's brother might be waiting for rescue as well; they just didn't know. He was depending on Max.

But all those children in chains. And Pricklestick had mentioned whips.

Lukas couldn't look at her. "I know I promised to help you find your brother. But I—"

"Just shut up," said Max. Emilie looked at her, shocked but speechless. "Seriously. Those are your friends down there. Carter wouldn't hesitate to help them, and I won't, either. So let's free them and get the heck out of there." She took a deep breath. The decision was made.

Lukas put his hand on her shoulder. "Thank you. And I know we'll have a better chance with you by our side."

"You bet," said Max, but the words came out stiff. She prayed she wasn't letting her brother down. "So what's the plan, then? Sneak into a camp of a few hundred rats and ogres and free their slaves with no one noticing? Easy."

Harold shook his head. Lukas and Emilie glanced around uncertainly.

"You want my opinion?" asked Pricklestick. "Humans are morons. Suit yourself, but there's no way me and Gud are going back down there among all them rats and ogres, no sir."

Slowly, Max felt a smile coming over her face. Judging by the look on Lukas's face, he was thinking the same thing.

"Pricklestick," Max said. "You may just be a genius."

The goblin did a double take and then started to wail.

❖

Despite Pricklestick's scathing indictment of their plan, it turned out that he would play a major role in its possible success. The cruel irony was not lost on the goblin as Max explained his part to him.

"You be wanting me to do what?" he cried. "That's not fair! All's I did was try and kill you, and now you're asking me to risk me own life?"

"Then we'll call it even," said Max.

"Do you know what would happen if they caught me helping you? Ever heard o' *gob ball*? That's playing ninepins with a goblin skull as the ball. And my skull is especially round, if you hadn't noticed."

"If you play your part right, they'll never even see you."

"And once we're finished, you're free," added Lukas. "You and Gud can return to terrorizing the Bonewood all you want. You have my word."

"Pish," said Pricklestick. "Your word! Everyone knows the only creature sneakier than a rat is a child."

Emilie gave the goblin a little shake. "Then help us, because otherwise I may just tie this sack up tight and toss it into the river, goblin and all. And maybe next time you'll think twice about waylaying innocent travelers."

The goblin whimpered but said nothing.

Max called their plan the Chewbacca maneuver after the scene in *Star Wars* where they rescue Princess Leia (Carter would have been so proud). The idea was for Max, Emilie and Lukas to pretend to be slaves, and for Gud to march them straight into the camp. Max and the others were already pretty dirty from days of hard travel, and it only took a little river mud to make them look really filthy. Pink hair would draw too much attention, so Emilie gave her kerchief to Max and helped her tie it up snug. It was strange to see

Emilie wearing her own golden blond hair loose. She winced as she ran muddy fingers through it until it was stringy and the color of spicy mustard.

"I wish I could come, too," said Harold as he watched the others grind dirt into their clothes.

"There's just no way to make you look like anything other than a trollson," explained Max. "Too big to be one of the slaves; not fat enough to be an ogre. No offense, Gud."

But if Gud took offense, he didn't show it. He rubbed his round belly and patted his head at the same time, and this accomplishment pleased him greatly.

Max patted her friend the trollson on the arm. "If we get into trouble, we'll be counting on you to get us out, Harold."

"*If?*" squeaked Pricklestick.

Emilie stuffed his head back into the sack.

"Give us half an hour to get inside the camp. Then you know what to do," said Max.

"You bet," said Harold.

"You don't have a watch, do you?"

Harold shrugged. "I'll count to eighteen hundred slowly."

Next Emilie handed him a small wooden box. "Here. When it's time, use this tinderbox. The grave moss should do nicely, but don't stand around too long to admire your handiwork."

"I'll be careful," said Harold. "You be careful, too."

"We will all be careful," said Lukas. "Careful and lucky, because we'll need both." First, he wrapped the Sword of the Eldest Boy in his cloak. Then he helped Emilie and Max tie lengths of rope loosely about their wrists, just tight enough to look like bonds but loose enough to shrug off if the need arose. They helped him loosely bind his own hands. Last, he reluctantly gave up his wrapped sword to Gud. "You'll have to carry that for us. We can't have slaves walking into camp armed."

The ogre sniffed the sword in his hands.

Lukas sighed. "Pricklestick, please make sure he doesn't try to eat it, okay?"

"Gud! No eat sword!" said the goblin from inside Emilie's sack.

"You'll have to keep your voice down once we get near the camp," said Emilie. "We don't want any rats asking to take a peek inside."

"We be doomed," whined the goblin.

With Gud leading the way, they began marching toward the eastern bridge. As they drew closer, Max looked across the river at the vast war camp assembled along the moors. Maybe they were doomed. But then, the Summer Isle was the place where the impossible became possible.

It was all about beating the odds.

CHAPTER FIFTEEN

O ne thing strongly in their favor was that if there was one species on the Summer Isle that didn't understand discipline, it was ogres. As Gud led the companions over the eastern bridge, Max was amazed to see how haphazardly spread out the ogres' camp was. Calling it a camp was actually generous—it had no real boundaries, no sentries posted or anything like that. Its defense was mostly "a bunch of ogres on the outside, rats in the middle."

Unfortunately, a bunch of ogres was deterrent enough. Those ranks of brutes would be the front line of the attack, but for now they milled about smashing each other with rocks for the fun of it and trying to eat things that shouldn't be eaten. Ogres applied a strict method to exploring the world around them: If you find something new, try to eat it. If that doesn't work, hit someone with it.

The slave children would be kept farther in, where they

could serve their masters without risk of getting squashed by a bored ogre. According to Pricklestick, the rats had put them to work making tools for the siege, and while the rats may not treat their slaves well, they didn't want them dead, either. To the rats, slaves were *property* and property had value.

As they approached the camp, Emilie whispered into Pricklestick's sack, "All right, goblin, we're almost there. Tell Gud to lead us to the children. Not to stop for anything."

Max could only hope the ogre had heard correctly. But as it turned out, he'd heard *too* correctly.

Things went smoothly at first, despite the foul conditions of the ogre camp. The snowy moorland had been trampled by scores of heavy feet until it was a muddy mess that threatened to suck the shoes off your feet with every step. The smell of rotting garbage lingered in the air, and worse, ogres weren't picky about where they relieved themselves. Max barely made it ten steps before she was openly gagging.

"It's working—just keep moving," said Lukas quietly. "Just breathe through your mouth."

Even that only helped so much.

"For once, I'm glad I'm in this sack," said Pricklestick. "I make Gud bathe monthly, I do."

Emilie shushed the goblin as she pinched her own nose shut.

The trouble came when another ogre crossed their path. It would have been easy enough to stop and wait for this other ogre to walk past, but unfortunately this was a situation where the simple, literal-minded Gud tried to do exactly as he had been told. He'd been told not to stop for anything, so he didn't. He barreled right into the oncoming ogre.

Two tons of fat and muscle collided. With a roar, the other ogre drew back a fist to plant a punch right between Gud's beady eyes. But Gud was still operating under his original instructions, and he wasn't stopping, even to defend himself. The other ogre wasn't expecting this, having never seen another ogre pass up the opportunity for a good brawl. He wasn't prepared when Gud simply shoved him out of the way and kept on walking.

Gud only made it another few yards before they heard the rumble of stomping feet coming toward them.

"Look out!" said Max, and the three children barely got out of the way before Gud was tackled from behind.

"Gud!" Pricklestick cried.

But the ogre was rolling around on the ground with his opponent, caught in a ferocious tangle of punching, kicking and biting. He was thoroughly enjoying himself.

Lukas snatched up his sword. More ogres were wandering in their direction to see what all the fuss was about. "Better get out of here!" Lukas advised.

Max, Lukas and Emilie fled toward the rats' camp. They walked as fast as they could without drawing attention to themselves. A few ogres looked up as they passed, but since they were headed toward the rats and not away from them, no one tried to stop them. They dodged past mounds of festering garbage until they spotted an enormous tent sewn from animal hides, in the dead center of the army. A flag flew overhead bearing a roughly painted rat's tail curling around a long knife.

The banner of the rat king himself.

Unlike the slothful ogres, the rats were busy. This camp rang out with the sounds of grinding as rats honed their bone daggers to razor-sharp edges. Smaller tents had been erected here and there, armories and food supplies. A line of rats practiced shooting target dummies with crude bows and arrows. Max could feel the tension in the air, the anticipation and bloodlust. They soon discovered what the rats had been forcing the children to work on as they came across racks and racks of freshly crafted tools, mostly crude axes. While the axes could be used in battle, Max suspected they were more for clearing the Deep Forest. They weren't simply going to invade the home of the elves; they were going to chop it down.

These rats were anxious for war, and they were well prepared.

"Have you ever seen rats so organized?" asked Lukas. "I hate to say it, but this new king of theirs must be clever."

Pricklestick was still thrashing about in his sack—he hadn't wanted to leave Gud behind.

"Gud's fine!" Emilie whispered. "But you won't be if you don't stop your foolish carrying on." She pulled her cloak over the sack so it wouldn't attract any more attention. "Please, Lukas, the sooner we free the prisoners, the sooner I can be rid of this goblin."

"We need to find where they're keeping the children,"

said Max. "They may be slaves, but the rats have to give them someplace to eat and sleep."

Lukas adjusted his sword to make sure the blade wasn't showing beneath its wrappings. "All right. We don't have Gud anymore, so pretending to be new prisoners isn't going to work for long. Keep your heads down and look for the children, but don't look like you're looking for the children. Look like you belong here."

"Nothing can go wrong with that plan," said Max.

"We're too far in now to turn back," said Lukas.

"I wouldn't want to," Max reassured him. "I just want to be ready for when it all blows up in our faces."

Lukas grinned and shook his head. "That's when we're at our best! Now, let's go before someone starts to wonder why three slave children are standing around whispering when they should be working."

They discovered that for the most part they were able to walk around the camp unchallenged. A few times some rat or another would grunt an order at them to fetch water. Once they were told to collect the spent arrows from the target range, and Max nearly became a pincushion as the rats opened fire again before she'd had time to get clear. They laughed at her as she scampered out of the way.

But they saw no other slaves. None at all.

"Maybe they're nearer the center of camp," suggested Emilie. "Closer to the king's tent."

Lukas frowned. "The guards there are going to be more alert. They might wonder why they haven't seen us around before."

"Ah, you children all looks the same," mumbled Prickle-stick. "Too ugly to tell apart."

"Let's hope the goblin is right, for once," said Max.

Together, the three of them (plus one goblin in a sack) made their way into the center of camp. As Lukas had expected, there were armed rats patrolling the perimeter, and guards stationed outside the king's tent.

They hadn't gone far before they heard a rat's gravelly voice snarling commands. "You lot! We need servers for the king's supper, so stand your filthy selves at attention or you'll get the lash!"

Max and Lukas exchanged a look. Who was the rat talking to like that?

Quietly, they followed the noise. Around the side of a supply tent they spotted the source. A massive wooden stake, easily half a foot in diameter, had been driven into the ground, and chained to that stake were at least twenty ragged children.

"Oh my God," breathed Emilie.

"It's them," said Lukas.

They were hardly children at all. The hollow expression on their faces, the hopelessness that weighed down their every movement made them seem more like objects.

"We have to get them out of here," whispered Max.

"But how?" asked Emilie.

"I don't know," said Max. "Yet. But we will."

As they watched, a large rat jabbed the butt of his pronged whip into the slaves' faces. "You, you and you. Attend to the king's supper." He raised the whip threateningly. "This time don't spill nothing!"

As a second rat used a ring of keys to unlock the children's chains, Max noticed that several of them had fresh red welts across their bare forearms.

The key ring...

"There," whispered Max. "See? He's the one we need to get."

Lukas and Emilie nodded.

The rat with the keys, the jailer, led the three children away. "To the pantry with you three, but don't get any ideas about stealing food for yourselves."

Lukas gestured for Max and Emilie to follow, and together they snuck around the back side of the tent and trailed the children from a safe distance. The children stopped outside a smaller tent guarded by two burly rats with mangy coats and many scars. The jailer grumbled something to the guards, and they stepped aside to let the children enter.

The jailer rat called after them. "His Majesty said not to skimp on the quail eggs."

"We need to get those keys," whispered Lukas.

"There's too many rats," answered Emilie. "Follow me."

The three of them crept around to the rear of the supply tent. Emilie took out a small knife from her belt and jabbed the blade into the animal-hide tent wall. Grunting with the effort, she cut a tear into the tent big enough to crawl through. "Keep a lookout," she whispered; then she slid into the tent.

Max's heart was racing. Emilie needed to hurry. Their cover as slaves wouldn't work if they were caught sneaking. She heard whispers from within. Then another voice, a harsh rat's squeak. Emilie cried out.

"There must've been a guard inside!" said Lukas. "Blast!" He yanked his sword clear of its wrappings, just as a commotion broke out around the other side of the tent.

Max turned in time to see another pair of rats running their way. "There!" one of them cried. "A child with a sword!"

"Run for it!" shouted Lukas as he brought up his sword to face them.

"Not without you and Emi—"

But Max was cut off as a clawed hand wrapped around her mouth and another grabbed her by the cloak. She was yanked, hard, through the slit Emilie had cut in the tent. She heard Lukas calling her name as she was thrown to the floor. She caught a glimpse of Emilie lying next to her. Rats' eyes glared down at her.

"Tie this one up, too," snarled the rat. "Then inform the king we have a new prize!"

CHAPTER SIXTEEN

They bound Max's wrists together so tightly that she couldn't feel her fingers. Beside her, Emilie was hauled to her feet by a rat clutching its bloody shoulder. "You'll pay for sticking me, child!" it growled.

So at least Emilie had gotten one good shot in before being captured. As the big rat with the whip dragged the two of them out of the supply tent, Max saw the child slaves watching them, their expressions inscrutable.

"Emilie?" said a gaunt boy with bright blue eyes.

"Marc?" answered Emilie. "Is that you?"

"Quiet, all of you!" shouted the big rat. "Slaves, back to your chains. You new lot, come with me."

As the rats marched the two girls through camp, Emilie whispered, "Lukas?"

Max shook her head. Lukas wouldn't have run off without them, which meant he went down fighting. She pushed the thought out of her mind. Lukas would be fine. He had to be.

"Marc," Emilie said. "He was the first Eldest Boy, but he's so skinny. I almost didn't recognize him."

"Where's Pricklestick?"

"I don't know. I dropped the sack when the rat attacked me."

Max certainly didn't like the little goblin, but she felt responsible for forcing him to come with them. Pricklestick was a mean creature, but he deserved better than being used as a gob ball.

They were taken to the rat king's tent, where the big rat with the whip spent a few minutes in conversation with the king's guards. Finally, he grabbed Max and Emilie by the scruffs of their necks and hauled them inside.

"Lukas!" Emilie immediately cried out as they saw their friend lying in the dirt. He groaned weakly in response.

The rat shoved Max and Emilie to the ground beside him. "Kneel in the presence of King Wormling, you maggots!"

Physically, this King Wormling was unimpressive. Max and her friends had fought the old rat king, Marrow, several times; he'd been a real monster—the biggest rat she'd ever seen. Wormling, on the other hand, was small and wiry, with a comically round belly. But his eyes shone with an intelligence Max hadn't seen before in a rat. Most rats looked at you with eyes full of greed or hunger. Not this new king.

This rat was studying them. And that scared Max more than Marrow ever had.

Escape was looking less and less likely. They were surrounded by a literal army of rats and ogres. Their only hope lay in Harold now. How long had they been sneaking around camp? An hour and a half? More?

Lukas's sword lay across Wormling's lap. The rat king ran his clawed fingers along the sword's black iron blade.

"I know this weapon," Wormling whined. His voice had the quality of fingernails dragged along a chalkboard. "The Sword of the Eldest Boy has drawn the blood of many rats over the years. Which means that I must have the honor of welcoming the Eldest Boy as my guest." His beady eyes darted to Emilie. "You know, my predecessors captured two Eldest Boys before this one, but I'm the first rat king to have the Eldest Girl as my prisoner. You are, aren't you?"

Emilie said nothing at first, but Lukas moaned again, semi-conscious. He had an angry purple bump on his forehead. "I need to look at his wound," she said. "It could be serious."

Wormling chuckled. "Look all you want, but your hands stay tied."

The big rat who'd brought them in, the one with the whip, leaned closer until Max could feel his breath on her face. "If it were up to me, you all wouldn't *have* any hands to tie. I'd be wearing your knucklebones around my neck."

"Then it's fortunate it's not up to you, Lasher," said Wormling. "Slaves without hands are just more mouths to feed."

"That boy took down three rats before we clubbed him," Lasher growled. "And the girl stuck poor Slinks in the shoulder."

But Wormling no longer seemed to be listening to the

other rat. His eyes were fixed on Max. "Before I became king, I did Marrow's listening for him. I was his eyes and ears in the world above, and he had me listen for talk of a child new to the Summer Isle. The last son of Hamelin. Marrow risked his throne, his life, to find him. Now Grannie Yaga has the whole rat kingdom preparing to make war on the elves for that very same boy. He's that important." Wormling leaned forward and planted the Sword of the Eldest Boy point-first into the dirt floor. "I wonder how important that makes his sister."

The rat king knew who Lukas and Emilie were, and he knew who she was, too. Max shouldn't have been surprised by this, but it was still startling. "I don't care about any of that *last son of Hamelin* junk. I just want my brother back."

"And that's why I caught you skulking around my camp? Were you looking for your brother, or were you trying to free *my* slaves?"

Emilie burst out, "They're people! You have no right!"

Wormling settled back into his chair. "I have the right of conquest. It has always been this way."

Lasher snarled at Emilie. Another outburst like that would get her beaten or worse, so Max decided to take a different tack. It was a long shot, but this rat king was a thinker, and that meant he might be reasoned with. Maybe.

"Actually, King Wormling," said Max, "we came here to negotiate."

Lasher's mouth twisted in confusion. "Eh? What's that?"

But Wormling's ears perked up.

"My king, they're making up words now to confuse us." Lasher held up his whip. "Let me teach them a lesson."

Wormling held up a hand. "No. Give me some time alone with them, Lasher. But don't go far. If I don't like what they have to say, I'll give them to you. For sport."

Lasher cast an evil look Max's way and then stepped outside.

"Now then," said Wormling. "To negotiate, you need to have something the other side wants. What could you possibly have that would interest me? What do you have that I couldn't simply seize by force?"

Max was taking an awfully big risk, but she'd remembered something the Peddler had said to them before they left Shades Harbor, that evil always turns on itself. Emilie was watching her, fearful that she would say something, the wrong thing.

"You're not a real king," said Max. "And you know it."

Emilie tensed up beside her. "What are you doing?" she whispered.

Wormling's voice turned hard and dangerous. He stood and lifted Lukas's sword over his head. "I wonder if the Sword of the Eldest Boy has ever tasted human blood."

"Because a real king shouldn't have to answer to anybody," said Max quickly. "Grannie Yaga tells you what to do, doesn't she? She put this army together to find my brother, but didn't you ever ask yourself why? You're smart—you must have!"

The rat king paused. "She said the boy was a danger to us all. She had foreseen it."

"But all we want is to go home."

Emilie looked up. She was catching on to Max's plan. "We want that, and to kill Grannie Yaga."

Wormling lowered the sword. "You?"

"We owe her that much," said Emilie.

"The witch is powerful," said the rat king, settling back into his chair. "She slew the Peddler in single combat, so how would a few children defeat her?"

"With that sword," said Max. "The Sword of the Eldest Boy was given to the New Hameliners by the Peddler himself, and it has the power to break her magic. Why do you think we're still alive? I've seen it work."

"Just a touch of the blade burned her," added Emilie.

Wormling lifted the sword and sniffed the blade. "There's something here, I'll grant you. Smells like the Peddler. Like his road used to before Grannie cut him down." He then turned his nose from the sword back to Max. "So say I believe you, and say I am tired of letting the witch tell me what to do. What's to stop me keeping the sword and killing her myself?"

Max took a breath and met Wormling's gaze head-on. "I think you're smarter than that. I think you know, just like we do, that even with that sword the odds are that Yaga would win any fight. She's that dangerous, and you're not like Marrow. I think you've gotten this far because you let others do the fighting for you."

Something like a grin passed over Wormling's face. "With that kind of thinking, you'd make an excellent rat."

Max let the uncomfortable compliment slide. "Let us go. Give us the sword back and let us leave with the others, and—"

"The others?" Wormling snarled. "You mean the slaves? Never. If I let you leave here with those children, the other rats would chew my ears to shreds. That would be the bloody end of King Wormling's reign."

"No one would have to know you helped us," said Max. "We could escape—"

"No," said Wormling. "Not a single slave gets freed today. Not ever."

And with those words Max's heart sank in her chest. There was a chance here that Wormling would allow the three of them to escape, if only to feed his own ambition to see Grannie dead and gone. But they were not walking out of there with the other children. Not with Wormling's blessing.

At that moment, however, Lasher came bursting through the tent door. "My lord! The ogres . . . the Bonewood!"

"Calm down, Lasher," snapped Wormling. "Take a breath and tell me what's going on. What about the ogres?"

"Sire, the Bonewood's on fire!"

Max could hear now, just beneath the sound of squealing, panicking rats, a low rumble. It sounded like a stampede was headed their way.

"The ogres are running to save their home," said Lasher. "The whole ogre army is on the move!"

Two hours. Harold had come through after all.

CHAPTER SEVENTEEN

Blackpaw carried Carter and Bandybulb high into the seaside cliffs, along narrow bluffs and winding trails where the winter winds blew in from the sea with enough force to knock over a stone troll. But the great she-wolf was surefooted and confident as she climbed, despite the added weight of her two passengers, and they were far less likely to encounter any more rat scouts along such precarious trails. Other than seabirds, they saw no creatures at all as the dense undergrowth of the valley gave way to spare patches of wind grass and lichen. At times, little more than a foot of rock was all that was between them and a plummeting drop into the frothing sea below. Still, Blackpaw never wavered from her course.

Carter wondered if the Piper's body was floating down there somewhere beneath the waves. But even as the thought came unbidden to his mind, Carter rejected it. The Piper wouldn't go so easily. If nothing else, he was a survivor; he would've found a way to survive that fall, too.

Magician's Landing grew ever closer. He could now clearly see the mile-long stone bridge connecting the small islet to the mainland coast. The bridge spanned treacherous coral reefs and breakers of stone, and atop the islet, the lighthouse glowed faintly in the gloom.

"This does not look like a place I'd choose to land my boat," said Bandybulb. "Even if I were a magician. Or had a boat."

"I think the magician's fabled landing was more like a shipwreck," said Blackpaw.

Carter gazed out over the endless black ocean crashing against the rocks. "It looks like the edge of the world."

Blackpaw stopped at a lichen-strewn cliff to let them all rest. "It is. Beyond that lighthouse is nothing but rough ocean. Are you sure you want to keep going?"

"I have to."

The wolf used her hind leg to scratch beneath her ear, but she said nothing. In the silence, Carter examined his own leg. His ankle was swollen and stiff, but at least he could flex all of his toes.

Please let it just be sprained. Please let it heal.

"Bandybulb, are you hungry?" Their provisions were running low, and Carter was down to dried nuts and berries. He produced a meager handful from his pocket.

Bandybulb accepted them with hearty thanks, but no sooner had Carter turned his head than the kobold was standing in front of him with his hand outstretched. "Seconds?"

Though a small creature, Bandybulb had a remarkable

appetite. Hopefully they could forage for food on the return trip. Of course, that was assuming they returned from Magician's Landing. That was no certainty.

While Bandybulb stuffed his face and Carter rubbed his sore ankle, Blackpaw padded along the trail, sniffing something in the wind. She let out a low whine.

"Is everything all right?" Carter asked. "Is it more rats?"

"Not close by," said the wolf. "But I smell smoke. The Bonewood is burning."

The Bonewood was many miles off, past the Deep Forest and on the other side of the Eastern Fork. Wolves had keen senses, but how could Blackpaw know about something so far away? In any case, the Bonewood was a hideous place.

"Well, can't say I'm too sad about it," Carter said.

"Yeah," agreed Bandybulb, spitting crumbs all down his front. "That place is nasty."

Blackpaw turned her golden eyes on Carter. "What about the Deep Forest? How did you feel when you set those trees aflame to free the Piper from the elves?"

Carter stopped rubbing his ankle. "What do you know about that?"

"I know that the Piper's new apprentice rescued him from the elves' justice," answered Blackpaw. "That he wielded magical flame to do so. The rats are hunting him, and now so are the elves. He is the second-most-wanted person in all the Summer Isle."

"Uh-oh," said Bandybulb.

Suddenly Carter looked at Blackpaw in a new light. Who was this wolf who'd saved their lives from the rats and who'd carried them this far? All of Bandybulb's warnings came rushing back to him in a flash. "What do you want?"

Blackpaw studied him. "I want to know why you have done the things you've done. The Piper is a villain. You have kept dangerous company, Carter."

Bandybulb began to whimper as he held on to Carter's leg.

Carter thought about trying to stand, but even before he hurt his ankle he'd have been far slower than Blackpaw. There would be no running from the wolf. "The elves were going to kill the Piper because of me. No trial. Nothing. That's not fair no matter what he's done."

Blackpaw's lips drew back in a snarl. "Fire is the tool of humans—the great devourer. And you brought it into my forest!"

Carter looked the wolf in the eyes. "Are you going to kill me for it?"

"If I said yes, what would you do? Would you use your magic to stop me?"

"Honestly, I don't know if I could. I'm . . . I'm not that good at it."

The growl died in Blackpaw's throat, and she sat back on her haunches. "I believe you. You are a reckless boy and you have much to answer for in letting the Piper live, but you are honest. Foolish, but honest, and that is what I came here to discover. I wanted to know if my first instincts about you were correct, Carter. I'm glad they are."

And then Blackpaw began to change. One moment she was a wolf, and the next a swirl of colors, of fur and flesh.

When it was over, Blackpaw was gone, and in her place stood an elf girl with nut-brown skin and leaves tangled in her hair.

"Leetha!" Carter exclaimed.

"Hello, Carter. Hello, Bandybulb."

The kobold ran to her and threw his little arms around her leg. She grinned and patted him on the head, and for a moment Carter wanted to hug her himself. The last time he'd seen her, her face had been so full of hurt, of betrayal, and he'd been so afraid that it would be his last memory of her. But just as quickly as his heart had soared upon seeing her, it sank again. It was his turn to be hurt.

"Why did you disguise yourself as a wolf?" he asked. "Why scare us like that? Why did you pretend to be Blackpaw?"

"I wasn't pretending," said Leetha. "When I'm the wolf, I am Blackpaw. Just as when I'm the elf girl, I'm Leetha."

"I don't . . . I don't understand."

Bandybulb quickly let go of his hug. "You're not going to turn back into a wolf now, are you?"

Leetha shook her head and sighed. "I needed to know whether you saved the Piper out of greed for his magic or whether it was something nobler. Stupid, but still noble. What you did was hurtful, Carter, and I had to know if I could trust you again."

"So you pretended to be the wolf so you could spy on me?"

"I didn't pretend to be the wolf. The wolf is as much a part of me as Leetha is."

"Wait a minute," said Carter, and this time he did pull himself to standing, as painful as it was. He wanted to look

Leetha in the eye. "You're not telling us everything, are you?"

"No. You see, Carter, if I put my trust in you again, it's not just Leetha I have to worry about, but my entire kingdom."

"Your . . . kingdom?"

She nodded. There was another swirl of color around her, and she transformed yet again. When it was over, she was still Leetha, but she stood taller somehow, more regal. Her hair had changed to silver, and her dirty tunic of woven leaves had become a dress that shone bright white against her dark skin. "But this is also who I am, Carter. I'm the Princess."

Carter didn't know what to say. Leetha, Blackpaw the wolf, the mysterious Princess of the Elves were one and the same, and had been for all this time. He held his crutch tightly so that he wouldn't fall over in shock.

Bandybulb looked at Carter and scratched his head. Then he squinted at the Princess and nodded.

"Knew it."

CHAPTER EIGHTEEN

eneath Carter was the raging sea. Behind him were deadly rats, witches and who knew what else. And somewhere ahead of him . . . what? The Piper? More dangers? He could barely walk. Carter knew magic yet couldn't control it. He was cold and scared and tired of adventures.

And all he could think about was whether or not he'd done or said anything rude in front of the Princess.

"You're . . . I mean, all this time . . . I'd better sit down."

"Here, Carter, let me help you." Leetha, the Princess, took him by the arm and gently helped him lower himself onto a nearby boulder.

"Your hair's silver," said Carter.

"When I want it to be. To tell the truth, I prefer it like *this.*" The Princess blurred, and in an instant she became the Leetha he knew, hair tangled with leaves and twigs.

Bandybulb kept closing his eyes, his face scrunched up in concentration.

"Are you feeling all right, Bandybulb?" asked Leetha.

"I am wondering if I am really King Tussleroot in disguise. You never know; I might have just forgotten!" The little kobold opened his eyes and waved his fat fingers in front of his face. "Hmm. Guess not."

"Why?" said Carter. "Why hide like that, Leetha . . . uh, Your Majesty?"

"Please, I prefer Leetha." The skinny elf girl–turned–Princess took up a handful of snow. "This is the longest winter in the history of the Summer Isle. I remember winters like this, back in the old world. Back before I led my people here. There, a long winter was hard but natural; it was part of the order of things. Here"—she crushed the snow in her palm and watched as it melted between her fingers—"the long winter is not natural. It's a sign of evil's triumph." Quickly she flicked the water from her hand and knelt in front of Carter. "And that, at least in part, is my fault."

"How could any of this be your fault? Who are you really?"

Leetha lowered her head like a little girl being scolded. "Can I be the Princess who doesn't want to be a princess anymore? The girl who runs from what she once was, who's willing to run with the wolves if it means getting away? Can I be all three?"

"Ah, yes," said Bandybulb, nodding sagely. "Now I am very confused."

Without warning, Leetha leaped to her feet and hopped up onto a rock overlooking the sea. It made Carter nervous to watch her stand so close to the edge of the drop-off, but she balanced there careless and confident. "I knew the Piper was dangerous. For years, I'd watched the Peddler's apprentice grow in power. First he rebelled, breaking the Peddler's rules and delving into places he'd been warned to avoid. Then he grew sullen, withdrawn. He'd always been a sly one, but now he turned sneaky. There were rumors that he'd even befriended witches.

"I'd warned the Peddler at the start that the boy didn't belong on the Summer Isle, and as my warnings came true, I was too proud to offer help. Let the Peddler deal with his wayward apprentice; I was not going to take sides in their feud. Not even when the Piper brought one hundred and thirty stolen human children to our isle. I was a fool, because one morning the elves woke up to find our own children missing. Every last one."

The Winter Children. Carter had seen the pain in Leetha's face whenever she talked about the children of the elves who'd mysteriously disappeared at the same time the children from Hamelin arrived. The elves blamed the Piper, and Carter had assumed that Leetha suffered from some kind of survivor's guilt because she'd been the only elf child left behind. But if she really was the Princess, it made sense that her grief would go much deeper than that—her grief, and her desire for vengeance.

Leetha continued without looking at Carter and Bandy-bulb. "Together the Peddler and I hunted down the Piper. When we found him, he fought us with everything he had. The boy had grown more powerful than either of us had an-ticipated, but he'd developed one weakness—his pipe. His music was his magic, and that flute of his had become his crutch."

Carter knew what Leetha meant, yet he couldn't help but be suddenly conscious of the wooden crutch beneath his arm. Without it, he was helpless. Was that how the Piper felt, deprived of his flute?

"The Peddler took the Piper's pipe away from him," explained Leetha, "and together we imprisoned him in the Black Tower. I argued for a harsher punishment, but the Peddler pleaded for mercy. For his part, the Piper stayed strangely silent. He didn't say a word as we closed the door to his cell.

"After that, I turned away. Turned my back on the human children, turned my back on my own people. I abdicated my throne and became Leetha, the elf girl who liked to wander and fight, who worried about no one but herself. Other times I was Blackpaw and I ran with the wolves. But I wasn't the Princess anymore. She stayed locked away in her castle, alone with her grief—or so the rumors claimed."

Carter remembered what he'd heard about the mysterious Princess of the Elves. Only that she'd retreated from view after she'd helped the Peddler imprison the Piper inside the Black Tower. No one in the Summer Isle had seen her in centuries. But that wasn't true at all—they just hadn't recognized her.

"Did anyone know?" Carter asked. "Anyone at all?"

"Outside of the elves? I think the Peddler knew, though he pretended he didn't. It was impossible to fool that old magician, and I suppose he thought it was a kindness to play along with my charade. He came to me, you know. Just before his death, to ask Leetha to plead with her princess for help in battling Yaga and the Piper. But he was really pleading with me. Even then, he played my game, but I answered his call too late."

"Do you think you could have saved him?"

Leetha shrugged. "I don't know. My powers have faded over the many years. I told you once, it's a terrible thing when an elf gives in to despair. Saps us dry, and so it has been with me. The Piper knew what he was doing when he stole the Winter Children away. He knew how much it would weaken me. The wound wasn't immediately fatal, but it's festered over time. I only have a little magic left. My days are spent as the carefree girl or the wolf. The Princess is hardly a threat anymore."

"Leetha, what if it wasn't the Piper who took the Winter Children away?"

"What are you talking about?"

"It's just that when I was with the Piper, he said that he didn't have anything to do with stealing the elf children. He said that Grannie Yaga must've done it to turn you against him."

Leetha scoffed at him. "Why would the old witch do that? They are obviously allies and have been for longer than anyone suspected. Didn't she turn you over to him? She used you to free the Piper from his prison!"

"I don't know, but if Grannie wanted you out of the picture that would be a good way to do it: fool you into fighting someone else while your powers were still strong, then sit back and wait."

"Carter, you have spent too much time with the Piper, and now you're starting to believe his lies. I can forgive you for what you did in the forest, for saving him, only because I know you did it out of some foolish sense of honor. But the reason I followed you as Blackpaw was to see if he'd corrupted you with his deceptions. So tell me the truth now: Whose side are you on?"

Carter threw up his hands. "You sound just like him, you know that? Maybe I don't want to be on anyone's side! Maybe I just want to go home."

Leetha watched him for a moment. She might have been an elf princess, but she still had the eyes of a predator. It was hard not to flinch under that stare.

"Carter, it's time for you to be honest with me—are you trying to stop the Piper or not?"

"I won't let him bring more children to the Summer Isle, if that's what you're asking. But I stand by saving his life—he's still the best bet I have of getting home. And besides that, it was the right thing to do."

In a blur, Leetha was Blackpaw again, and she trotted over. "I think you're a fool boy, Carter, but for what it's worth, I'm glad we're on the same side." She bent down beside him. "Climb on. We still have a long way to go, and time grows short. Even if we continue to avoid the witch, we can't let the Piper beat us to Magician's Landing."

"You think he's still alive, then?"

Blackpaw let out a low growl. "For the time being. But we should hurry."

Carter climbed once more onto the wolf's back.

Bandybulb hopped up, too, and gave Leetha a hug. "You see? I knew she wasn't going to eat us."

CHAPTER NINETEEN

Everywhere she looked, Max saw squealing, fleeing rats. Wormling's tent had been flattened in the stampede of ogres. The Bonewood was on fire, and the dumb, lumbering beasts stomped on anything that stood in their way, be it tents, rats or—if Max wasn't careful—pink-haired girls.

Only the Bonewood wasn't on fire, not really. As part of the plan, Harold had gathered damp clumps of grave moss, piling them along the edge of the forest. When the time came, he'd used Emilie's tinderbox to set the piles aflame. Lots of smoke, very little fire. And they were lucky that the wind was blowing southwesterly today, carrying the smoke into camp and starting the panic.

As obnoxious as Pricklestick was, he'd been right about one thing—ogres were homebodies. It was this love of home that normally kept the rest of the Summer Isle safe from their rampages, because as a rule ogres didn't venture far from their beloved Bonewood. It had only been recently, under the direction of Grannie Yaga, that they had started to roam far and wide. But now, with the Bonewood threatened, the ogres ran en masse for home.

Harold's ruse had worked so far, but it wouldn't take long for even the dim-witted ogres to figure out that there was no real danger. Even now, the first of them were crossing the Eastern Fork. Lukas was on his feet, though still dazed from his fight with the rats, so Max took him by the arm and led him through the chaos. Emilie ran alongside, carrying the Sword of the Eldest Boy.

"Did you see Wormling?" Max asked.

Emilie shook her head. "When that ogre came barging into the tent, he scurried away. Didn't even stop long enough to pick up the sword. A real instinct for self-preservation that one has."

They were headed for the slave pens when an ogre barreled past. Max had to yank Lukas out of the creature's path as it stomped by them, through the supply tent, and out the other side. He left a trail of smashed quail eggs in his wake.

"So much for the king's supper," quipped Max.

On the other side of the supply tent, they came to the slave pens. The children were huddled together around the massive post that held their chains.

"Emilie!" called one of the boys. "And Lukas!"

"Marc, we've come to get you out of here."

The boy's face lit up with hope, but quickly darkened again as he held up the stout chain connecting his collar to the thick post. "The rats made us forge our own chains. Without the keys we'll never get free."

"Where's the jailer?" asked Max.

But Marc hadn't seen him. Of course, the rat could be anywhere in all this confusion. Now what were they supposed to do? The diversion had worked perfectly—but if they couldn't free the slaves, then it would all be for nothing.

"You, girl! I figured I'd find you here."

Max turned to see the big rat named Lasher stalking toward them. He had his whip at the ready and teeth bared in an ugly sneer. Lukas was still woozy and in no condition to fight.

"Emilie, give me the sword," said Max.

The girl looked at her for a moment, then handed it over. "You're sure about this?"

"Nope," said Max. "You just figure out a way to get those chains off!"

Max held the sword in both hands and stepped forward to face the rat. The sword was much heavier than it looked, and didn't have nearly the reach of the spear she'd lost in the river.

Lasher cracked his whip. "They say that King Marrow died fighting a girl much like you."

"Not much like me, it *was* me."

"They also say that she won because someone else stabbed Marrow in the back."

"Yeah, but only because she beat me to it." That was a lie, because if Leetha hadn't killed Marrow, Max would probably be dead herself. But every second she kept this rat trash-talking was a second she stayed alive.

Lasher hissed as he struck with his whip, and left an

angry red welt across Max's cheek. She touched her cheek lightly, and her fingers came away bloody.

So much for trash-talking.

Max edged herself sideways to draw Lasher away from Emilie and the other children, even as she kept the sword held high.

Lasher followed her with the whip, testing her, toying with her, and Max only barely managed to avoid any more cuts. Around them the turmoil was starting to quiet down as the rats began to drag themselves out of hiding after the ogres' charge. Max was only dimly aware of Emilie shouting nearby—she was arguing with someone—but she didn't dare take her eyes off Lasher long enough to see who it was.

The rat lunged forward, but the lunge turned into a feint as he sidestepped and brought his whip around for another attack. But Max met the feint with a charge of her own, swinging the sword in a wild arc over her head. It was luck as much as anything that brought her sword around just ahead of Lasher's whip crack, and before the startled rat could adjust, Max's blade left a clean cut along Lasher's chest.

It wasn't a deep wound, but it hurt. The rat squealed in pain and outrage as he brought his whip around again. Only this time, he wasn't aiming for Max. Lasher's whip wrapped tight around the sword blade, and then the rat yanked, hard. After a brief tug-of-war, the sword went flying out of Max's hands.

Max was unarmed.

Frantic, Max looked around for a weapon—a stick, a rock, anything—but there wasn't so much as a pebble.

With an evil chuckle, Lasher stalked forward. Whip in

one hand, sword in the other. "Think I'll keep this as a trophy. Along with your bones . . ."

The rat's boast trailed off as his gaze drifted from Max to something else, something behind her. Max barely registered the shadow in time to leap to the side, out of the way of the massive shape coming toward them.

Lasher let out a cry, but he wasn't quick enough to escape the enormous boulder that came hurtling from the sky. It landed with an almost comical *thump,* and where there had once been a rat there was now just a rock embedded in the dirt. Only Lasher's fallen weapons, and a few inches of tail, remained visible.

A familiar little voice laughed. "Rat pancake!"

Max looked up to see Gud looming over her. Pricklestick perched atop the ogre's shoulders, leering at their handiwork.

Once Max was sure the goblin wasn't planning on making *her* into a pancake, she snatched up the Sword of the Eldest Boy and searched for Emilie. The other girl was trying to calm the slave children, who were still chained to the post. Lukas was standing on his own now, and looked a little less bleary-eyed than before.

"Where did they come from?" asked Max as she gestured back to the goblin and ogre duo.

"After Pricklestick escaped the sack, they must've reunited in all the chaos," said Emilie. "I saw them wandering the camp and made them an offer if they helped us."

"What offer?"

"Duke Pricklestick."

"Huh? You can't make anyone into a duke! You're Eldest Girl, not queen—"

Emilie shushed her with a finger to her lips. "You and I know that. *They* don't."

A great cloud of dust had been kicked up during the ogres' stampede, but that was now beginning to settle, and more and more rats were becoming curious as to what children without chains were doing near the slave pen. Small groups were starting to wander in their direction, and they didn't look friendly.

"Not that I don't appreciate the save, Emilie, but we still don't have a way of freeing the children!"

"I've thought of that." Emilie whistled to get Pricklestick's attention, and the goblin turned Gud in their direction. "We need your help over here."

The goblin folded his skinny arms defiantly across his chest. "You need my help, *what?*"

Emilie sighed. "We need your help, *my lord* Pricklestick."

The goblin beamed at them. "Me likes the sound of that!" He urged Gud over to them.

"The post, please, my lord," said Emilie.

Gud reached down and grabbed the wooden post staked deep into the ground. He heaved, and the post gave a little but didn't come free. Annoyed, Gud looked at it and growled. Then he bent low, putting his back into it, and the brutish ogre yanked the post clear of the frozen earth.

The chains wrapped around it slid free. Though still locked in their slave collars, the children were no longer tethered to the post.

"Quickly now," said Emilie. "Gather up your chains so that you don't stumble on our way out of here. We'll have you out of those collars eventually, but for now, let's go! Back to New Hamelin. We'll get you home, I promise."

Max glanced warily at the gathering rats who were by now surrounding them. "Pricklestick! Can you clear us a way out of here?"

The goblin scratched his chin. "What's in it for me?"

"Oh, come on . . . Emilie?"

"Fine," said the girl. "*Baron* Pricklestick, Lord of the North Hamelin Reaches. Will that do?"

The goblin smiled broadly. "Done!"

"The North Hamelin Reaches?" Max whispered.

Emilie shrugged. "Sounds like it's a thing, doesn't it?"

Then, with a roar, Gud began stomping toward the Deep Forest, swatting any unfortunate rat that got in his way. Emilie led the freed slave children after him, and Max and Lukas brought up the rear. The rats were still too shell-shocked and disorganized to put up much of a fight. One look at Gud, and most ran squealing.

As they cleared the camp and made for the trees, Max looked across the river at the distant Bonewood for any sign of Harold. It was hard to see through all the smoke, but a few ogres, having realized that their home was in fact not on fire, were wandering back to the camp. Most look confused, some angry. A few punched each other for fun.

With Harold's help, they'd just freed the children who'd been stolen from New Hamelin and forced into slavery. And they'd rescued them from under the noses of an army of rats and ogres.

Max grinned. *Score one for the good guys.*

But then, without warning, a shadow passed overhead, and Max felt an all-too-familiar shiver creep down her spine.

"The witch!" Lukas pointed to a long-necked bird

circling overhead, squawking and honking at the pan-icked rats.

The rats began to fall into line. Gud continued to punch a path through the crowds, and Emilie hurried the freed children along behind him, but rats everywhere were stopping their retreat. A large group of twenty or so began to gather, closing ranks to bar the children's escape.

"We're not going to make it," said Lukas. A rat appeared out of the billowing dust, and he knocked it away. "We need another distraction!"

Frantically, Max looked everywhere until she found what she was looking for—the target dummies that had been used in bow practice. Several of the bows lay abandoned on the ground.

"Here, take this." Max gave the sword to Lukas, then snatched up two bows. "Emilie, head for the far side of the river and find Harold. Get these poor kids out of here and don't stop!"

"What about you?"

"Carter's still out there somewhere, but we'll catch up when we find him. Now go!"

Emilie grabbed Max in a quick hug. "You'll find him," she whispered. Then she wrapped her arms around the shoulders of two slave children who were barely strong enough to walk. "Move! Keep going!"

Lukas appeared at Max's side. "What are you doing?"

"Help me!" she said. "Grab some arrows!"

Lukas grinned when he saw what she was planning. "You ever use one of these before?"

"There's so many of them it's going to be hard to miss!"

Lukas sheathed his sword and picked up a bow. "Like this!"

Max cocked an arrow and drew it back.

"One, two, fire!"

They let their arrows fly into the growing crowd of rats trying to block the children's escape. Max's bowstring caught her on the wrist. "Ow!"

"Look," said Lukas. "One of us got one."

A rat lay in the dirt with an arrow protruding from his still form. The rest were in a panic, looking for where the deadly arrow had come from.

"Again!" said Max. Together they fired another volley, and both arrows struck home.

This time, however, the rats spotted Max and Lukas and, with a squeal of delight, charged forward.

"Come on!" yelled Lukas, and the two of them ran, dodging past tents and more startled rats. They zigzagged here and there, leading the rats away from Emilie and the rest of the children.

"We're doing it!" panted Lukas as they sprinted past a row of rat-king banners that had been trampled by stampeding ogres. "They're following us instead of the children!"

"Yeah, but where are we?"

Max paused and stole a quick glance over her shoulder. She could hear the pursuing rats drawing near, their hisses and squeals getting louder with each passing second. But none of the tents looked familiar. Everything looked exactly the same.

They were lost in the middle of the enemy camp.

⟨ CHAPTER TWENTY ⟩

Storm clouds brewed in the distance, but they were no ordinary clouds. They swirled dark and heavy over the Deep Forest, a black hole in the purple sky of twilight.

"Grannie Yaga is finally beginning her attack," said Leetha, coming to Carter's side. The three companions were approaching the final leg of the cliff trail, a narrow path of stone steps that wound five hundred feet down to the rocky beach that ringed the bridge to Magician's Landing.

The storm over the Deep Forest grew violent as forks of lightning cut through the sky. A bolt struck a tree below with a crash.

"You want to be there, don't you?" asked Carter.

"Our borders are not as defenseless as some think. If the witch wants to do battle with the elves, she will have a tough fight on her hands." She looked at Carter, her expression grave. "But I will feel every blow that lands, every tree that falls—and still I choose to be here with you."

"Why?"

"She's searching for you in the wrong place, but it won't be long before the witch realizes her mistake. Grannie Yaga hunts you for a reason, Carter. That alone is proof that your story isn't over quite yet, and I want to make sure it ends the right way."

"Which way is that?"

Leetha broke out into a mischievous grin as she wagged her finger at him. "You humans—always wanting someone to spoil the story for you. Where's the fun in that?"

As she bounded off toward the long steps, she was suddenly the Leetha he knew—the sly elf girl whose sense of humor veered to the dangerous, to say the least.

It wasn't necessarily a welcome change. Carter had the familiar feeling of being part of a plan no one had shared with him. Like he was being manipulated yet again. The victim of forces beyond his control.

No. Carter had made the decision to go to Magician's Landing on his own. If Leetha had plans that coincided with his, then fine. If not, he wouldn't allow himself to be led astray. He'd find the Piper's magic pipe. He would use it to get himself and the children of Hamelin home again. The Summer Isle could fight its wars without him, thank you.

The stairway down was especially difficult for Carter, more so because the sun had nearly set and the steps were hard to see in the dark. Carrying the two of them up the bluffs had exhausted the seemingly inexhaustible wolf, so Carter insisted he and Bandybulb walk in order to give her a chance to rest. Leetha still wanted to reach the beach below before making camp for the night, so she led the way in elf-girl form. Carter took each precarious step slowly and carefully, while Bandybulb worried at his side the entire way.

Thankfully, he reached the bottom without any major falls, and as the last sliver of pink twilight disappeared they made camp. The ever-present danger of rat scouts meant they couldn't risk a campfire, so they huddled in their cloaks amidst a circle of lichen-covered boulders and nibbled on a meal of nuts and berries. Carter put his swollen ankle up and tried to work out the knots in the rest of his tired muscles. Besides the throbbing ankle, the rest of his body was beginning to protest the unusual strain brought on by walking with the crutch. But they were familiar pains Carter had lived with for most of his life . . . pains he'd thought he was free of.

Meanwhile, Bandybulb was saying something about the great nautical exploits of King Tussleroot, but Carter wasn't listening. He closed his eyes instead and tried to focus. He tried to push all the distractions away, just like the Piper had taught him. He also had to push away the stab of anger when he thought about his former teacher, but soon enough he was calm and intent on his own breathing.

Dig deep, Carter, the Piper had told him. *Where does your strength come from?*

The rocks, the beach, even the oceans here were touched by magic. In his mind's eye, Carter could picture Leetha and Bandybulb, and the elf girl glowed with a powerful aura of green, but where the aura should have been blooming, it wilted with guilt. There was magic all around, a million possibilities all interconnected. What happened here on this little beach affected the sea, the wind and even the distant lighthouse they were headed for. Minuscule repercussions went by mostly unnoticed, but if the strings were pulled in just the right way, those tiny repercussions could become a tidal wave. Possibilities would be blown wide open, and anything could happen. All it took was a magician.

Carter had failed so many times. The Piper hadn't bothered to hide the disappointment in his face—not ever. And yet, there had been times—when the Piper thought Carter wasn't looking—that Carter had seen something else there, too. A flash of something closer to . . . wonder. Wonder at Carter, the boy who'd spent his life apart. Like the Piper, Carter had had to work harder than everyone around him just to keep up.

Use the magic, the Piper would say. *Defy the odds. Do what everyone else thinks is impossible.*

It was as if he were standing there whispering in Carter's ear:

It's what makes us the same, Carter. Because it's what we've done our whole lives. Me without a family, you with your leg. Yet we survived, we succeeded in spite of everyone.

We have always been magicians, because our whole lives we have been about defying the odds.

Only the Piper had one piece of the puzzle wrong. The very first time Carter had done magic on his own, when he'd lit a simple campfire, he hadn't been thinking about his anger. He hadn't focused on the people who'd stared or made fun of him.

He'd been thinking about the people who'd supported

him. His parents. His sister. The Piper was wrong, because Carter hadn't survived on his own, and there was nothing weak in that.

"Carter, are you okay?"

Bandybulb's voice sounded far off. Carter could barely hear him because he felt like he was floating in a sea of possibilities. He knew this place where chance was stacked against him, because he'd lived there his whole life. What were the odds that a boy with a clubfoot, who endured endless taunts at school and stares from strangers on the street, would grow up with confidence and pride? What were the odds?

Not that bad if you had someone to help you along the way.

With his friends and family in mind, Carter went back to one of the Piper's most basic lessons, but one that Carter had never mastered. In his mind's eye he reached out and tugged at the strings of chance. He imagined Max's hand on his shoulder, gently urging him along.

A simple bit of magic, the Piper had said. A test every magician needed to pass . . .

"Carter!" Bandybulb was saying. "You are missing the best parts of my story about King Tussleroot and the queen of the mermaids— Oh, my!"

Carter opened his eyes and looked at Leetha and Bandybulb. But neither of them was paying him any mind. They were too focused on the object that had just appeared out of thin air—a perfect, still-warm cherry pie.

❈

The pie was a huge success: sweet and tart, with a flaky crust. Even Leetha, who was not one for compliments, admitted it tasted delicious. Bandybulb had dug into the pie with relish and finished two-thirds of it all by himself. Now the poor kobold lay on his back moaning in misery as he rubbed his overfull belly.

For the first time since his original conjuring of a campfire, Carter's magic had worked exactly as intended. He couldn't stop smiling.

Leetha studied him curiously as they ate. "You conjured this pie without any aid?"

"What do you mean?"

"The Piper uses music as his magic. That's why he's so desperate to get his pipe back, because he's bonded with it in such a way that no other replacement instrument will do. Even the Peddler's magic was tied to his road."

"Yeah," said Carter. "The Piper mentioned something like that. He said I needed to find my thing, but I guess I just don't have one."

"No wand, staff, anything like that?"

"Wand? No. Is that stuff for real?"

"Hmm."

For a moment, Leetha just watched him, until Carter began to feel uncomfortable under her stare. He didn't know why.

"So," he said, trying to change the subject. "Speaking of the Piper's pipe, do you think it's close by?"

Leetha nodded. "Some say the lighthouse on Magician's Landing is the oldest structure in all the Summer Isle, left here by forgotten gods to light the way for those seeking sanctuary."

"Sounds like as a good place as any to hide a magic flute."

"We are nearly there. The worst may be behind us."

"Do you really believe that?"

The elf girl shrugged. "No. I was only trying to be positive. You humans are always so stupidly optimistic that I thought you'd appreciate the effort."

There was that elf straightforwardness again, or *rudeness* might be a better word. Or was she teasing him? Carter never could tell with Leetha, but he realized that in their time apart he'd actually come to miss it. The Princess was intimidating, the wolf somewhat frightening, but he genuinely liked the girl. Carter chose to believe that of the three, the girl was the truest part of her.

In any case, Carter was feeling bolstered by his achievement. He might limp to the finish line, but he would do so as a magician. Or at least a conjurer of pies.

Now that night had fallen, the lighthouse was the sole light in the darkness—a signal fire marking the edge of the known world. Up close, the bridge didn't inspire much confidence. Pockmarked with age and crumbling in places, it looked treacherous at best. The crashing of waves breaking against the bridge was the only sound. In the darkness, Carter could just make out the shapes of what looked like enormous piles of stones, placed like markers along the bridge every thirty feet or so.

"Burial cairns," said Leetha, noticing Carter's interest. "Many must have died building that bridge."

"I thought you said it was built by forgotten gods or something."

Leetha grinned. "Why do you think they were forgotten?"

Bandybulb summed up Carter's feelings succinctly. "This is not a good place."

"This is where the last boat from the old world came ashore," said Leetha. "It carried only two passengers. One was human; one was not."

"The Piper and the Peddler," said Carter. "But the Peddler wasn't human?"

Leetha shook her head. "The Peddler was no more a man than Grannie Yaga is a woman. He was an immortal, a force of nature. He was the Peddler."

"I never knew."

"It's an important distinction. The Summer Isle was never meant for humans, Carter. So you can imagine my shock when the Peddler appeared with a young man in tow."

"You were here?"

Leetha's gaze drifted to the pebbled beach. "I was waiting in this very spot. The waves dashed the boat against the rocks, and it splintered. I pulled the young man ashore." She was quiet for a moment. Then, "I should have let him drown."

"How can saving anyone ever be the wrong choice? If you had let the Piper die, what would that have made you?"

"I would be a princess who hadn't lost her people's children." With a sigh, Leetha stood up and brushed the sand off herself. "I'm going to scout ahead." Then Leetha transformed herself into Blackpaw. "That bridge will be treacherous in the dark—" she started to growl, but broke off in midsentence.

The crash of waves had been joined by something else, a harsh chorus of caws overhead and the frantic flapping of wings.

"Are those crows?" asked Bandybulb.

Blackpaw lifted her snout and sniffed the air. "Carter, get down!"

Carter was knocked backward onto his rear as Blackpaw leaped atop him. He heard a twang, then a yelp as an arrow struck Blackpaw just above her right foreleg. The wolf tumbled forward into the sand.

A thousand needles stabbed his injured ankle as Carter rolled over it, but he ignored the pain as best he could. He pushed himself up just in time to see the dark silhouettes of two rats emerging from their hiding places among the rocks. One wielded a fearsome spiked club, and the other was nocking a second arrow. Their eyes gleamed in the darkness.

"Finish the wolf," snarled the one with the club to his companion. "Then we'll chuck the kobold into the sea. The crows can fly ahead and tell King Wormling we have the witch's prize!"

Blackpaw whined as she tried to stand and failed. The second rat drew back his bowstring and aimed the arrow.

Time slowed. Carter heard Blackpaw's whimpers, the cawing of the crows overhead and the breaking of waves against the shore. It felt like those sounds would go on forever, like he was stuck between heartbeats because he was terrified of what was about to happen next.

It had taken a great deal of time and focus to conjure a pie from thin air, because such a thing was impossible in the real world. But there were many more possibilities that could alter the situation he was currently in, possibilities that existed and only needed a little push to become real. A far subtler magic but one just as effective.

Carter pushed.

There was another *twang,* but instead of the arrow taking flight, the bow's crude string snapped, sending the arrow off uselessly in the wrong direction. The rat squealed as the bow whacked him in the face.

"Fool!" his companion hissed. "I'll finish it."

He hefted his club and stalked forward. It would take more than a weak bowstring to stop him, but Carter was feeling confident. Where magic was concerned, he was now two for two. Their lives were on the line, and it was time to go big.

"Get behind me," he said to Bandybulb. Then he planted himself between the rats and Blackpaw.

The flap of a butterfly's wings can cause a hurricane on the other side of the world, Carter thought. *I can do this.*

Carter moved his fingers, plucking at the invisible strings of magic only he could see. What started as a breeze swiftly became a gale of wind blowing sand and pebbles into the air. Bandybulb covered his head.

The sand stung Carter's eyes, but he didn't let it break his concentration. The rat cursed and snarled against the biting winds but kept coming forward.

Carter needed more. The rats were coming at him head-long, facing the wind. Each step was a struggle, but each step brought them that much closer. Just a few feet away and still Carter couldn't stop them. Carter pushed, sending wind and sand howling at the rats. One of them fell to all fours, desperately clutching at the beach to keep from being blown away. The bigger one dropped its club but did not fall. Another step.

The rat was in a wind tunnel but did not falter.

Another step and it was just a foot away. The rat snarled, baring yellow teeth as it leaned in, struggling to stay upright against the wind.

Every muscle in Carter's body burned with the effort to keep the gust blowing.

Another step. The rat opened its mouth wide . . .

And squealed as it was lifted off its feet. It slammed into its companion as the two of them were blown up over the beach, over the waves and far, far out to sea.

Carter sank to the ground as if punched in the stomach. The air knocked out of him, his head dizzy, he worried that he might pass out.

But he'd done it. The Piper had summoned the wind several times, and now so had Carter. There wasn't time to congratulate himself, however. Despite the dizziness, Carter pulled himself to sitting and looked for Bandybulb and Leetha. She was her elf-girl self again, and the kobold was gently examining the arrow protruding from her shoulder. Blood stained her front.

"It is deep," the kobold said.

"Let me," said Leetha, through gritted teeth. The elf girl wrapped a trembling hand around the shaft and, with a scream, yanked the arrow free. Then she fell backward, spent. Her eyelids fluttered weakly as she threatened to faint.

Carter gave up trying to stand—his legs felt like rubber—and crawled over to her instead. "We need bandages to stop the bleeding." Using Leetha's knife, he began to tear strips of cloth from his cloak.

Without warning, the crows above began to let out a terrible caterwaul. They circled overhead for a few moments and disappeared past the cliffs.

"Spies," said Leetha, barely holding on to consciousness. "Grannie Yaga will soon know where we are."

Carter sped up his work as he continued to cut strips of fabric from his cloak. "Here, start tying these over the wound."

Bandybulb worked fast. His chubby little fingers were surpassingly nimble. In just a few minutes they had Leetha's shoulder wrapped tight. Hopefully it would be enough to stop the worst of the bleeding.

"She's hurt bad," said Bandybulb. "Can we use magic?"

Carter hesitated. "Healing magic is tricky. I'm not sure if I can."

"Too dangerous," said the elf girl. "I'll heal in time."

Leetha was breathing easily now, but her normally ruddy brown complexion was pale from blood loss. Still, she was determined to walk. And she was right, they couldn't be here when Grannie Yaga showed up.

"I'll help you," said Carter.

Leetha arched her eyebrow at him. "You can barely walk yourself."

"Then we'll help each other. C'mon."

With Carter's aid, the elf girl managed to stand on wobbly legs. She swayed unsteadily for a moment.

"Carter," she said. "What you did with the rats . . ."

He grinned. "Yeah, I wasn't sure it would work."

Leetha looked directly into his eyes. "Be careful. I do not mean this as an insult, but you are only human."

"What do you mean? For the first time, my magic's working the way it's supposed to."

"There's a danger. The Piper uses his music as his focus . . . channels magic through his pipes. And you . . . remember what happens when he tries to summon too much?"

Carter nodded. "The pipe usually shatters."

Leetha pointed a finger at his chest. "Carter, you are the pipe."

He didn't understand. For once he was doing things right; the magic was working. "Are you saying I'm going to . . . what? Hurt myself?"

But instead of answering, Leetha sagged. Her eyes fluttered again, and this time they stayed closed.

"Put your arm around me," said Carter. "I'll lean on the crutch, and you lean on me."

"Carter . . . ," she murmured.

"I know, I'll be careful. No more big magic. Just save your strength, okay?"

Leetha nodded, and the three of them set off along the ancient bridge toward the lighthouse, which now looked more distant than ever. It would be excruciatingly slow going, with Leetha having to rest often and Carter's ankle throbbing with the extra strain, but at least they were moving.

And all the while, Carter kept thinking about Leetha's warning. For a happy few minutes, he'd felt like a real magician. But now whenever he thought about magic, all he saw was the Piper's prison cell, and the floor covered in splintered pipes.

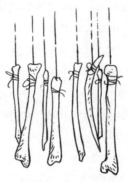

CHAPTER TWENTY-ONE

They'd lost the rats somewhere between the mounds of ogre dung and boiling skulls. At least, Max hoped they'd lost them. Or else the rats were being really, really sneaky. Either way, whatever part of the camp Max and Lukas had wandered into, it was unlike anything they'd seen. Or ever wanted to see again.

There were no tents here, only piles of bleached bones stacked up next to boiling cauldrons. Everyone knew that rats hated fire and would not go near an open flame, so whoever was tending those cauldrons, it wasn't a rat. Max didn't have to look inside to know what the cauldrons contained—someone was boiling the flesh off the bones of the rats' dead.

Max and Lukas proceeded carefully, steering clear of the cauldrons but staying on the lookout for rat patrols.

"They have to be looking for us," Max whispered.

"Yeah, but it's gotten quiet; have you noticed? Hopefully that means Emilie and the children made it safely across the river."

Max nodded as she checked the jars in her backpack. They were still securely wrapped up. Max couldn't forget that she was responsible now for her parents' lives as well as her own. They needed a way out of the camp and to safety. But she had become so hopelessly lost, they could be walking ten feet from the river and she wouldn't even know it. They needed higher ground to get their bearings.

She pointed to a hill just past the gruesome bone piles, and they began to make their way closer.

What they found stopped them in their tracks. A hut stood atop the hill, overlooking the field of bones. The shingled roof slanted to one side, and the doorway and front porch were decorated with bone chimes that rattled in the blowing wind.

"She's rebuilt it!" Max gasped.

They'd stumbled upon Grannie Yaga's hut.

Lukas stared at it for a long minute, then took a step forward.

"What are you doing?" Max whispered. "Let's get out of here!"

But the boy shook his head as he drew his black iron sword. "I swore I'd kill that witch. For Paul."

"Lukas—" Max began, but the boy cut her off.

"And not just Paul. Yaga said herself she was after Carter, and if there's even a small chance I can stop her here, shouldn't I take it? We may not get this chance again!"

The smart thing would have been to explain to Lukas what a macho idiot he was being. The smart thing would have been to turn and head back, to find their friends and not risk their lives fighting a powerful witch face to face. But the smart plans had rarely worked. It'd been obvious for some time now that they were heroes by the seats of their pants.

"Stupid boy," Max muttered. "Fine. We'll do it together. And don't you dare try and talk me out of coming with you!"

"I gave that up a long time ago. Only, this time do stay behind me, okay?"

The bone chimes rattled in the wind. A flickering fire-light lit the windows like two demonic eyes watching them. Max and Lukas stayed low and out of the view of the front window until they were up against the hut itself.

Carefully, slowly, Lukas peeked over the edge of the window into the hut. After a few moments he knelt back down.

"It looks empty. But there's a fire in the hearth, so she'll probably not be gone long."

"So we leave?"

Lukas shook his head. "No. We wait inside, and when she comes back we ambush her. We'll have a better chance with surprise on our side."

"Okay, but just in case, I'll open the door and cover you," said Max. "That's what they do in cop movies."

Lukas gave her a confused look.

"Never mind. Just stab anything that looks witchy."

The porch creaked ominously beneath their footsteps, causing Max to cringe. The last time they'd seen Yaga's hut, it had been walking around on giant chicken legs, and Max suddenly wondered if it could do those things when Yaga wasn't controlling it. Was it alive somehow? And if so, would that mean they were basically stepping into its mouth?

Max tried to put the thought out of her mind. This was just a hut like any other. A hut that sometimes grew giant chicken legs.

The front door was unlocked. On the count of three, Max threw open the door and Lukas rushed inside.

After a second Lukas called, "Come on, it's empty!"

If the bone chimes outside Grannie's hut were creepy, they were nothing compared to the inside. Dried herbs hung in bundles from the ceiling, but so did shriveled corpses of bats, toads and other small creatures. A cauldron bubbled over a small fire in the hearth, and a broom (of course) rested against the far wall near a dark alcove that held a dirty-looking cot. But by far the most ominous thing in there was the extra-large iron oven, with a door wide enough to fit a person—two if they were children. Even more unnerving was the fact that the oven *locked from the outside*.

Thankfully, the oven was cold.

"Look at this place," said Lukas.

Max wrinkled her nose. "*Smell* this place."

"Let's find somewhere to hide. Then when she enters we—"

The words died on Lukas's lips as something in the shadows, or maybe the shadow itself, stepped forward. At first Max stood there in shock—she didn't understand what she was seeing, how darkness could take solid shape. Then the creature became clearer, and Max recognized the bony arms, the shriveled skin barely concealed by layers of rotting and tattered rags—a gray man.

Lukas leaped into action and swung his sword at the creature. He connected with a crack of bone and brittle flesh, but the gray man barely reacted. Whatever magic the sword possessed, it couldn't hurt a creature that was already dead.

Lukas and Max stumbled backward, away from the nightmare creature. It placed itself between them and the door, blocking their escape.

But it came no closer.

"What's it doing?" gasped Max.

But Lukas shook his head. He'd gone white, and the Sword of the Eldest Boy shook in his shivering hands.

Max took another step back, and started as she nearly stepped into the fireplace. The gray man drew closer and then retreated.

"It's the fire!" said Max. "Remember? The one in the Black Tower couldn't stand the light. I bet they're afraid of fire!"

"What are you doing?" hissed Lukas.

"Cover me!" Max ran for the broom in the corner.

The gray man reached for her, but Lukas swung his sword, raining a flurry of cuts across its emaciated chest. He managed to slow the creature down, but the wounds didn't hurt it.

Max shoved the straw end into the fire. Arms out, fingers clutching, the gray man brushed Lukas aside just as Max withdrew the broom, which was now a flaming torch. The gray man reared back as Max shoved the burning brand into the creature's face. The instant the flames touched those dry, brittle rags, the entire thing went up like flash paper. A bright flare of flame, and then the gray man was nothing but charred pieces of cloth drifting through the air.

"Stories say the gray men hide in shadows where they can't be seen until the sun goes down," said Lukas. He stepped to the window and peeked out. "This one must've been protecting Grannie's hut. The moon's rising, and . . . Wait, there's someone coming this way."

"Is it Yaga?"

"Maybe." Lukas gripped his sword tight. "But she's not alone. There's at least four of them."

"That's too many," said Max.

"I may not get another opportunity like this!"

"It won't matter if you get us both killed!"

Lukas punched the wall in frustration. "Well, what are we supposed to do? We can't exactly hide in the shadows. If Yaga catches us, we'll be as good as dinner!"

"Wait," said Max. "That gives me an idea. Come on!"

Reluctantly, Lukas gave one last look over his shoulder and hurried toward her. Max stashed the burnt broom behind a table and opened the enormous oven door. She sure hoped this was a good idea. "Quick, get inside."

"Are you insane?"

"It's the last place she'd think to look! Now get in the oven!"

Lukas looked ready to keep arguing, but at that moment there was a loud squeak as someone stepped on the loose board just outside the door. Max shoved Lukas toward the oven, and together they crawled inside. It was a very tight fit, and they were covered in the ashes of Max-didn't-want-to-imagine-what. She left the heavy door open just a crack and wedged the blade of her knife into the hinge so that they wouldn't get accidentally locked in.

"This is the worst idea ever," whispered Lukas.

Max shushed him, but she worried that he might be right.

The front door to the hut opened, and the sound of the wind blowing outside picked up to a howl.

"Grannie, do you want to hear my news or not?" said a familiar voice. "The crows have been talking."

"Still eavesdropping on birds, are you, rat king?" answered the witch. "What do you know?"

"A human boy was seen traveling with a kobold and an elf girl. The boy walked with a crutch."

Max's heart jumped. *A crutch? It has to be Carter!*

Grannie obviously thought the same thing. "Where? In the Deep Forest?"

"No," answered Wormling, who sounded like he was enjoying this part. "They were spotted along the coast, headed south."

"When was this?"

"Not several hours ago."

Grannie began pacing. "South along the coast? Why wouldn't Carter seek protection from the elves? Unless . . ."

"What? What is there along the coast other than rocks and sea?"

"Tsk, tsk, such a naughty boy to be so clever! Magician's Landing is where he's headed, or I'll eat my own thumb."

"Never heard of it."

"Magician's Landing is where they came ashore, the Peddler and the Piper. Of course, it makes the story complete, don't it? That's where the sentimental old fool would've hid the Piper's pipe, and it explains why we ain't heard from the Piper in so long. They're racing for it!"

Lukas leaned close and whispered, "We have to stop her!" But Max shushed him again. She was working on a plan.

Meanwhile, Grannie barked orders at the rat king. "Forget the elves for now. Round up your army, because tonight we march south to Magician's Landing. We'll take the Peddler's Road. Now that the old magician is dead, there's no one to stop us using it, and it cuts right through the forest. That's how we'll find the boy. That's how we'll find victory!"

"You want me to simply call off the attack? What about the escaped slave children? My camp is in shambles!"

"It doesn't matter anymore. The boy's not in the Deep Forest."

"I promised my rats spoils of war. All I've done so far is lose their slaves!"

"Thanks to your dear Grannie, you now command the most vicious horde this isle has ever seen, rat king. After tonight you'll have your pick of the place; you can sack and ruin as you desire—the Deep Forest, even New Hamelin. No one will be able to stand up to you. But it all hinges on this night!"

"Why? What's happening?"

Grannie laughed again. "The end game! All the players gathering on the same spot, now. Tonight, we finish it! Do as I say, rat king. Don't make me repeat myself."

There was the sound of shuffling, of bowing bodies as the rats excused themselves and the door opened and shut behind them.

"Now," Lukas whispered. "She's alone."

But Max shook her head. Their vengeance would have to wait a little longer.

Through the crack in the oven door, Max could just see the hem of Grannie's dress as she settled into her rocking chair. The witch banged her cane against the bubbling cauldron three times. "Let's go!" she cried. "Double time to Magician's Landing!"

Suddenly the floor lurched. The walls creaked and jars tumbled from the table as the hut lifted itself off the ground. But they weren't flying. Max knew what was happening even if she couldn't see—the hut was standing up.

Then they were moving. Grannie's enchanted hut ran on long legs through the forest, while Grannie hummed a little song.

"What's going on?" whispered Lukas, but Max found his hand and gave it a squeeze.

"It's all right," Max whispered back. "She's taking us to Carter! Once we're with him, then we deal with the witch."

Max and Lukas held hands tight as the hut bounced and jostled all around them, and the oven ash and soot stung their eyes and tickled their throats. But at last Max was on her way to fetch her brother. She'd promised to find him, and she would keep that promise even if it meant stowing away inside Grannie Yaga's oven.

PART III

MAGICIAN'S LANDING

The march to Magician's Landing was a hard road to travel. Not for Grannie and the walking hut, and not for the rat horde trailing in its wake, but for two children bouncing around inside a giant oven it was torture. Lukas could hear the rats' squeals of delight as the hut stomped along the Peddler's Road. Elves in the trees harried them along the way with arrows, but Grannie flung curses from her high perch and sent the defenders retreating for the safety of the deeper forest. Lukas imagined gray men hunting the shadows for those either too slow or too foolhardy to flee with the rest, and he tried to put the gruesome images out of his mind.

Unsurprisingly, ovens were not built with travel comfort in mind, and Lukas ended up banged and bruised by the constant jostling of the hut's jerking movements. But despite it all, Max insisted that they wait. Grannie had to lead them to Carter; then they would handle the witch. So Lukas sat tight as the moon outside reached its zenith and began its trek down again. Past the witching hour into the hours of early morning.

In time, the horde fell behind. Not even the fleet-footed rats could keep up with Grannie's long-legged hut. Grannie Yaga was driven to reach Magician's Landing with no time to spare.

Which was just fine with Lukas. The sooner, the better. He only hoped that when it came time to fight, he wouldn't be too stiff and sore to actually do anything. As it was, he'd spent most of the trip rubbing the feeling back into his cramped legs.

At last the hut came to a stop. Lukas listened for any sounds of movement from within, but all he could hear was the wind and the waves of the nearby sea.

"Maybe she's asleep," Max whispered.

Lukas doubted it. He'd never been so lucky.

Slowly, ever so slowly, he eased open the oven door. The fire had died down to a pile of smoldering embers and the room was dark. Though it was difficult to make out in the mostly lightless room, Grannie's rocking chair sat motionless next to the hearth. The chair was turned with its back to Lukas and the oven. Perhaps they'd caught the witch napping. Wincing against the protestations of his cramped muscles, Lukas pulled himself free. As quietly as he could, he drew his sword and tiptoed closer to the rocking chair. One step. Two.

Behind him, someone sneezed. Lukas whipped around to see Max with her hand over her nose and mouth, trying desperately to hold a second sneeze in. It wasn't going to work.

As the second, even louder sneeze came, Lukas charged Grannie's chair. He didn't pause to take aim; he simply drove the point through the back. It cut through and out the other side. But wood was all his blade found, because when he turned the chair around, it was empty.

"She's not here." He yanked his sword free. "Which is probably for the best, considering all the noise you just made."

"It was all that soot," said Max, rubbing her black nose. "I've been holding it in all night long!"

Lukas peered out the window. "Speaking of night, shouldn't the sun be up by now?" The Winter Moon was still high in the sky, and there wasn't even the faintest glimmer of pink on the horizon.

"Maybe it's earlier than we think?"

Lukas doubted it. The days had been getting shorter and shorter ever since the Peddler's death, and it seemed that at long last, the sun wasn't going to rise at all. The Summer Isle was becoming what they feared—a land of eternal night. By moonlight they could see the whitecaps of an ocean breaking against the sides of a long stone bridge stretching from the shore out to sea. At the far end of the bridge, a light burned in a high tower. "That must be Magician's Landing."

"So we made it. That's one problem solved, at least."

"But now we have another," said Lukas as he pointed out the window to the beach far below.

"You're kidding me! This thing's still got its legs out?" Max turned around and said, "Hut, sit!"

"I don't think it'll listen to us. Look around for some rope, or anything we could use to climb down."

They stirred the embers of the dying fire and, by that weak orange glow, hunted through Yaga's hut for anything that could help them reach the beach below. That search was one of the most unpleasant tasks Lukas had ever done. The bits of things floating in jars were bad enough, but some of them actually moved when you got too close. Things that, separated from their bodies, shouldn't move ever. But in a basket hidden in the corner, Max found a coil of well-worn rope and two pairs of child-sized shackles.

"What do you think she has in mind for these?" Max asked.

"We don't want to know," said Lukas. "Drop the shackles and grab the rope."

They tied one end of the rope to the leg of Grannie's heavy oven and dangled the other over the side of the hut. It reached the ground with length to spare. Lukas went first, shinnying down the rope as it swayed precariously. A fall from that height would be bad enough, but the ground below was jagged with rocks. When Lukas reached the bottom he held the rope still for Max.

"I never could climb the rope in gym class," she said, out of breath. "That was intense."

Lukas had no idea what she was talking about, but he nodded anyway. Max and her brother often spoke of things that were totally alien to Lukas and the rest of the New Hameliners. He'd discovered long ago that it was easier to just nod rather than ask them to explain.

"Keep an eye out for Yaga," said Lukas. "She has to be

around somewhere, and remember, if she tries to curse you, stay close to me and the sword."

"You know, if you just let me have the sword for little while . . ."

Lukas gave her a look that was unmistakable even in the dark.

Max held up her hands. "Just asking."

It wasn't that Lukas didn't want Max to have the sword's protection against the witch, and if it had been a talisman he would have handed it over to her gladly. He would have insisted that she carry it. But it wasn't a charm or a trinket; it was a weapon, one whose sole purpose might be to destroy Grannie Yaga. If so, Lukas needed to be holding it when it struck the killing blow. For Paul.

Side by side they approached the bridge to Magician's Landing. Lukas stopped at the foot of the bridge and bent down to examine the ground. His fingers came up wet. "Blood."

A look of panic flashed across Max's face. "Let's hurry."

They continued for a few minutes without talking, listening instead for voices or footsteps, but it was hard to hear anything besides the roar of the waves crashing below. Before long they encountered piles of stones, some of which were taller than Lukas. In the dark, it felt like the stones were watching Lukas and Max as they passed by. Every now and again, Lukas would stop as he spied fresh drops of blood that shone black in the moonlight against the sun-bleached stone. Whatever wounded creature they were following, it was close.

Lukas and Max had just rounded a narrow stretch of

bridge bordered on either side by steep drops and rough sea when one of the nearby cairns moved. No, the stones didn't move; rather, someone stepped out from behind them. Her hunched silhouette was instantly recognizable as she emerged from her hiding place.

"So the hunter becomes the hunted, eh?" said Grannie Yaga. She squinted down on them with her one good eye. "I can smell the blood, too. Wonder who it belongs to. Dear little Carter, perhaps? I'll soon find out!"

Lukas didn't wait to see what the witch would say next. With the Sword of the Eldest Boy held aloft, he ran at her. He had two thoughts in mind—one, to draw Grannie's attention away from Max, and two, to get to the witch before she had time to cast a spell. In the first, he succeeded, but in the second . . . Grannie had learned since their last encounter not to bother trying to curse Lukas directly. This time she leveled her magic at his surroundings instead.

With a cackling cry, she waved her bony fingers, and Lukas heard a loud *crack* just as the stones beneath his feet shifted. A ten-foot chunk of bridge, including the stones Lukas had been standing on, split loose and began to tumble into the sea. Lukas managed to roll clear, but in doing so he dropped the Sword of the Eldest Boy. It skidded along the bridge and into the waiting ocean below.

For a moment Lukas couldn't think about the crumbling stones, or the witch, or the dark sea waiting to swallow him up. All he could think was, *I've lost the Sword of the Eldest Boy.*

He saw a flash of pink scurrying after it. What was Max doing? The waves would crush her against the rocks below like an egg against a pan.

Lukas managed to hang on as the rumble of sliding stone below him ended with an enormous splash. His back and legs were soaked by the freezing spray of salt water, but still Lukas clung to the bridge. Inch by painful inch he pulled himself back onto solid ground, and as he did so he caught a glimpse of Max. The Sword of the Eldest Boy hadn't fallen into the sea after all; it was caught on one of the balusters supporting the bridge from below and dangled precariously over the waves. Max was climbing down, her arm stretched wide, as she tried to rescue the precious blade.

"Trying to save his nasty little sword, dear?" Grannie had spotted Max as well. "Not before I freeze your heart in your chest!"

Lukas scrambled to his feet as the witch pointed a clawed finger at Max.

"*Switch, witch, buckle or brew,*" she sang. "*Brother's in the oven, so I choose you.*"

"No!" Paul had died because he'd been hit with a curse meant for Lukas. The Peddler had died protecting them all. Grannie wouldn't get Max, too. Not her.

He threw himself between Grannie and Max, and the witch's killing spell hit him like a winter's gale. The air in his lungs turned to frost as the curse stole through his blood, hunting for his heart.

Lukas's heart stopped beating as he crumpled to the ground. The last thing the boy heard was Max calling his name.

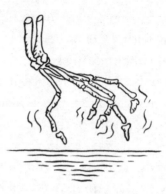

CHAPTER TWENTY-THREE

Grannie stopped laughing. "Eh?"

Max pulled herself up onto the bridge, the sword clutched in her hands, just in time to see Lukas let out a gasp. His eyes closed.

"Lukas, no!" Max gripped the sword tight as she ran toward them.

Grannie pointed her bony finger, and a blast of frigid air hit Max in the face. It robbed her of her breath, but then the sword grew warm in her hands and the cold vanished.

Grannie roared in frustration. "I'll not need my magic to eat your heart raw, little girl!" But the witch dared not come closer to the sword.

Max reached Lukas and put an ear to his chest. Nothing. Grannie's curse had stopped his heart. Lukas's face was already turning blue. Ignoring the witch, she straddled him and pressed both hands over his chest. She pushed. She pushed again. *Three, four, five . . .*

One of the things about growing up with a younger brother like Carter was that her parents had made sure Max learned CPR as soon as she was able. It had taken Carter years longer than the other kids to learn to swim, and even today he was still always falling down, tripping over his brace. Poor, clumsy kid . . .

Twenty-eight, twenty-nine, thirty.

Max watched Lukas's chest for a sign of breath. Her biceps were already shaking from the effort.

Nothing.

She put her mouth over his and blew. More compressions. *One, two, three . . .*

Lukas let out a little gasp as his eyelids fluttered open. "Oh . . . Ouch."

Max grabbed his head and hugged him close, her tears smearing their soot-stained cheeks.

"Where's Grannie?" he whispered.

As if in answer, the witch called out, "I'm done playing with you children!" Max saw now that as she'd been trying to resuscitate Lukas, Grannie had been seeding the ground with small white objects no bigger than . . . *knucklebones.*

Max knew what was coming next. She'd seen this trick of Grannie's before. "Come on!" She tried to pull Lukas to standing, but the boy was too weak to move. The knucklebones sprouted into skeletal hands. On their fingers, they skittered like spiders.

The sword! Max reached for it, but one of the bone hands

gripped her wrist, pinning it. Her arm twisted the wrong way, and something in Max's shoulder threatened to pop.

"Now look at you two," said Grannie. "You're both scrappers, I'll give you that. But I'm not about to let you interfere with my little reunion with your brother. I expect I'll find him around here somewhere."

"I'm here," called a familiar voice, and from the shadows a few yards down the path stepped a boy leaning on a primitive crutch.

Carter! It was him. Max's brother was here. After all this time he was here and all Max could do was wish he would go away. She tried to shout at him, but the words wouldn't come. *Run! Run! Don't you see that Grannie's here for you? Run away!*

But of course he couldn't run. That was the one thing her brother had never been able to do.

"Carter!" Max finally managed to shout. Her brother's eyes flicked to his sister for a second, and in that look she saw joy, confusion and fear. Of course, he'd thought she was safe and sound back home. Didn't he know she would come for him? She would always come for him.

"Hi, Max," he said, but he was looking once again at Grannie. Hesitantly, he stepped forward.

"Carter, my dear," said the witch, grinning. "That's it. If you want your sister to live, you'll come to your Grannie without fussing. My hut's waiting, and you've got to take your medicine like a good boy."

He took another step. "I'm not going with you. So just let my sister go."

The witch's smile faded. "Cheeky mouth on you, boy. But we'll see how stubborn you are with your head on the chopping block! The sun's down for good. Now I just need to snuff out one last candle, and that's you, boy. Less painful if you do as I say. Come with me and at least I'll give your friends a running start." She extended her finger at Carter. "From now on, no child leaves my Winter Isle. Not ever."

Max cried and strained against the bony fingers holding her down. And the sword was so close, just inches from her grasp. "Carter!"

She watched as her brother closed his eyes and took a deep breath.

"What're you doing, boy?" asked Grannie. "Making peace with your maker?"

"No," said Carter simply. "I'm focusing."

Grannie cocked her head. "Eh?"

Carter opened his eyes, a look of furious concentration on his face. His fingers played with something invisible in the air.

The witch burst into flames. She lit up like a bundle of dry kindling and let out a horrible cry as she ran, thrashing at the flames as she went. Grannie Yaga leaped from the bridge and disappeared into the dark sea below.

CHAPTER TWENTY-FOUR

C arter had just finished telling Max his story for the first time (he'd end up telling it several more times before Max even began to understand how her little brother of all people had learned to throw fireballs) when an odd creature stepped out from behind his legs and bowed. It was squat and made Max immediately think of a furry potato wearing pants.

"I am Bandybulb, and it is a pleasure to meet you!"

Max shook the odd little creature's hand. Then the four of them took shelter at a spot Carter had chosen, where two collapsed cairns formed a shallow cave. Leetha was already inside, sleeping beside a tidy driftwood fire. Her shoulder was wrapped in blood-soaked bandages, but she was breathing regularly.

Max helped Lukas into the little cave, but he refused to lie down. Though too weak to stand on his own, he insisted on keeping watch. He shivered despite the many cloaks they'd wrapped around him—a lingering effect perhaps of Grannie's curse. Nevertheless, the Eldest Boy sat huddled in his cloaks, staring out at the dark sea.

"You should lie down," said Max. "We're out of danger."

"Are you sure?" He glanced at her but swiftly turned his attention back to the water.

"You saw what Carter did to Grannie. She's toast, no pun intended."

"I've seen that witch take an arrow to the eye and shrug it off. We shouldn't let our guard down."

"Captain Lukas, sir!" The little creature appeared at his side, beaming up at him. "You look much worse than the last time we met!"

"I know."

"Much, much worse. You know, King Tussleroot always says that if you are dying, it's polite to give others ample warning."

"Uh, you two know each other?" asked Max.

Lukas nodded and offered a slight smile. "All too well. Bandybulb is a kobold."

"He's been a big help," said Carter.

"Really?" asked Lukas.

"Yeah," said her brother. "I know what you're thinking, but he has."

Lukas shook his head. "Another bit of magic, I suppose."

The little kobold cocked his head and peered up at Lukas. "Are you cold?"

"I'll be fine."

Then Bandybulb took off his own little cloak and tried to wrap it around Lukas, but the kobold-sized garment was so small, he only ended up covering Lukas's left foot.

"How are you now?" asked Bandybulb.

Lukas laughed, seemingly in spite of himself. "My foot is much warmer, thank you."

With a satisfied nod, the kobold plopped down next to him. "What are we watching for?"

"Witches."

"Ah, good." The kobold paused, then whispered, "I hope we don't spot any."

Max took this opportunity to pull Carter aside and talk privately. "So you do magic now, huh?"

Carter held out his hands. "I dunno. I guess so."

"Cool."

Her little brother was a magician. Carter's story of his adventures after escaping the Black Tower was harrowing and thrilling, but nothing he said could compare to what she'd seen with her own eyes—he'd conjured fire from thin air. At first Max hadn't been sure that this was the same boy she'd grown up with, and there was a seriousness about him that hadn't been there before. The Summer Isle had changed them both, but not so much that they weren't quickly back to their usual banter.

"And you led an army to rescue New Hamelin from an army of rats and ogres?" asked Carter.

"Sorta."

"Also cool." Her brother was quiet for a moment. "I mean, it's not like *doing magic* cool or anything, but—"

Max punched him in the arm, just hard enough to hurt. He winced. "Ow, you still hit like a girl."

"You mean hard enough to knock your head off?"

"Yeah, something like that."

Carter leaned against the rocks and rubbed his injured ankle. Max sat next to him.

"How's it feeling?"

"Better. The isle heals things."

Though she didn't say it out loud, *wouldn't ever* say it out loud, Max wished she'd been there to see her brother run without the brace. Even just once. Maybe she'd still have the chance.

"Max," said her brother, after a moment, "can I see Mom and Dad?"

She knew this was coming. Of everything, this had been the hardest part to tell him. Max had barely been able to get the words out, and she hated hearing herself say it. *Our parents are cursed, their souls trapped in glass.*

But Carter had heard the truth, and now he deserved to see for himself. She carefully removed the bundle of cloth from her backpack and unwrapped the two jars on the ground in front of her brother. Carter picked up one jar, then the other, and held them up to catch the moonlight. Their parents' faces floated there, sleeping. As peaceful as always.

"You said the magician who did this to them is dead?"

"Yes," said Max. "He got stomped on by a very big troll."

"Good."

Max didn't like to hear her brother talk that way. He'd never been a grim boy before the Summer Isle, and she didn't think it suited him now. She wondered then if the Piper hadn't taught him more than just magic. Would it ever be possible to unlearn those lessons?

"Only a magician can safely break the curse," she said.

"I hope you don't mean me." Carter gently replaced the jars in Max's backpack. "The best I've been able to do is conjure a cherry pie."

"And the fire," said Max. "We all saw that."

"You were in danger. I know it sounds corny, but you and Mom and Dad—you guys help me focus. The magic's easy then."

"Doesn't sound corny. Sounds like family."

Her brother was quiet for a moment. "Max, do you think Grannie's really gone?"

Max looked out at the water. Black waves crashed against the rocks. "If the fire didn't get her, then the ocean had to, right?"

"Lukas doesn't seem to think so."

"Lukas is a pessimist."

Carter glanced at her. "Since when?"

That was a good question. When had poor Lukas become so defeated? This journey had changed them all, and not entirely for the better. The Summer Isle might have been a dreamland once upon a time, but now it was cold and brutal. Max couldn't help but think of all those Border-towners who'd followed her here. What sort of life could they carve out for themselves in a place like this?

Max took Carter's hand gently in hers. "You know I came back here to take you home, Carter."

"I know." Her brother squeezed her hand. "And I'm

ready to go home. Just run away from all this, but . . . it isn't finished."

Max rubbed her eyes. He was right, and she hated it when he was right. "No. It's not."

"The Piper." Carter pointed up to the lighthouse, not so far away now, but more menacing than ever. The signal fire up top seemed to be staring down at them like some glowing eye. "I think he's waiting for us."

"But Lukas can hardly hold his head up. Leetha's in no shape to help. And Bandybulb's . . . Bandybulb."

"Hello!" As if on cue, the kobold offered a good-natured wave from his seat inside the little cave.

"That fight with Grannie took it all out of us, Carter."

"Not all of us." Carter shifted his crutch. "There's you and me."

"You can barely walk—"

"I told you I'm getting better. And you can help me, anyway."

"What if Grannie's *not* dead?"

"Then I'll handle her."

Max studied her brother.

On really bad days, the days when the two of them had fought from dawn to dusk, Max would often ask her parents why they had ever decided to curse her with a little brother. What in the world had she done to deserve such a lifelong punishment?

Her mom and dad would smile, shrug and say, "We didn't do it for you, sweetheart. But someday you'll thank us for it, anyway."

She hated it when her parents were right.

"Come on, then," said Max. "Let's tell the others and make it quick. Goodbyes suck."

❖

Beyond the lighthouse at Magician's Landing was nothing but rough ocean. The Sea of Troubles went on for many thousands of miles. And farther still was the end of the world.

The lighthouse was far enough for Max.

"You're sure the pipe's in there?" asked Max as they stepped off the bridge onto the rocky islet upon which the lighthouse was built.

"I think it's a pretty good bet," answered her brother.

Max grasped the Sword of the Eldest Boy tight, testing its grip for the twentieth time. Lukas had insisted that she take it, and when she balked, when she complained that Lukas would be powerless against Grannie should she attack again, Lukas cut her off with a single whisper.

"Grannie's not after me," he'd said.

Lukas was right. If taking the Sword of the Eldest Boy meant that Max might have a better chance of protecting her brother, then she'd take it. They'd left their friends in the little cave, where Bandybulb was quite serious about his job as nurse. He'd even managed to make Lukas rest, threatening to recite King Tussleroot's Daily Instructions to Achieve a Healthful Long Life if he refused. When Lukas learned that the instructions numbered in the many hundreds, he quickly complied.

Carter and Max would come back for them, and all five

companions would march out of Magician's Landing together. That was the plan and the promise.

"Well, there's only one way to find out if the pipe's in there." Carter shambled forward on his crutch. Max offered to give him a hand, but he'd said he wanted to enter the lighthouse on his own. He had a feeling, as he was sure she did, that the worst was yet to come.

"You know," said Max as she followed close behind, "I don't think the name *Sword of the Eldest Boy* really fits anymore, do you?"

"*Sword of the Pink-Haired Tween?*" joked Carter.

"I was thinking of renaming the sword something a little more me. How about *Bad News?*"

Carter looked over his shoulder at her and grinned. "Perfect. I feel safer already."

Max's brother was such a good liar.

They circled the base of the lighthouse until they found themselves between the tower and the shore. A narrow flight of steps led up to an open, oval archway. Carter let Max help him up the steps, but he froze as they started inside.

"What's wrong?"

"Nothing. It's just . . . the last time I went inside a tower, it didn't end so well."

"The Black Tower and the Piper's prison?"

"Yeah."

Max clapped him on the back. "You're a big-time magician now! Nothing's going to touch you."

Carter nodded, without much enthusiasm. "What about you?"

Max patted her sword. "Anyone messes with me, I got Bad News for 'em. Let's go."

The interior of the lighthouse was plain sea stone, much like the outside. A curling staircase climbed the walls, and torches, burning in sconces, lit the way.

"Someone's home," said Carter.

"Wow, you know it is creepy how much this place looks like the Black Tower. You think that's a coincidence?"

"I think the Summer Isle has another word for coincidence."

"What's that?"

"Magic." Carter started up the stairway, his crutch echoing off the floor with every step. "I think you're going to have to help me."

Max put an arm around her brother. Carter winced as his swollen ankle brushed against the stone. "Does it hurt much?" she asked.

"Yeah. But I'll deal."

"Here, lean more on me."

They made their way like that, step by step, until they came to an open door. The wind could be heard outside, and the flicker of the lighthouse's bright flame cast long shadows in orange light.

Max nodded to her brother as they emerged onto a roofed stone platform. Four sturdy stone pillars held up the ceiling, but the walls were open to the air. The stone floor simply ended at a drop to the rocks and sea far below. In the center of the floor was a large stone brazier, and inside a brilliant fire blazed. The lighthouse's watch fire.

A slim, hooded figure stood there staring into the flames, his cloak of red, green and yellow blowing in the wind.

There was no kindling of any kind feeding the fire. Instead, burning at the heart of the blaze was a delicate musical pipe.

CHAPTER TWENTY-FIVE

Now they were reunited, Carter and the Piper, apprentice and teacher. Having come all those miles together, having fought and argued and saved each other's lives, they'd reached their destination at last.

Just to watch the Piper's pipe burn.

"I've been thinking about mirrors," said the Piper, still staring into the flames. He hadn't even looked at Carter and Max.

Max leaned over to Carter and said, "He's still crazy, right?"

"Most of the time, yeah."

The Piper continued, as if he hadn't heard them. Or simply didn't care. "Take the mirror in my prison cell, for instance. It was a gift from Grannie, you know. Well, I've been thinking about what she wanted me to do with it."

"What was that?" asked Carter. The wind blew harsh and strong up here, and he had to raise his voice to be heard.

"She showed me you. She taught me the secrets of the mirror, how I might use it to cast a spell into your world, even if I couldn't physically reach there myself. I watched you grow up. I waited for you. Waited and watched."

"Then you kidnapped us."

The Piper waved his hand. "You know I hate that word, Carter. But fine, call it what you want. What matters is that the mirror could be used not just as a window, but as a door to another world."

He gazed out over the night sky, his face shrouded in the depths of his cloak. "That got me wondering what *she* did with it—Grannie, I mean. All those years in her possession, and what was the witch up to? She obviously never went through the mirror herself because, as your sister found out, the mirror is a one-way trip. From within my prison I was able to cast my song through the mirror and enter your dreams. And like the children of old, you followed the Piper into the mountains and woke up in a land of magic.

"But Grannie doesn't know the secret paths between our worlds like I do. All those years with the mirror in her possession, and all she could do was watch. Must've driven her mad."

Then he turned to face them, and Carter saw the Piper hadn't escaped his fall from the cliff unscathed. Quite the opposite. Every breath he took seemed to hurt, and he held one hand protectively over his ribs. There was dried blood staining a tear along his right pants leg. His patchwork cloak, though tattered and torn, hung loosely from his shoulders. He was lucky to be standing at all.

"Why are you going on about your stupid mirror?" asked Max. "It's over. Your pipe is burning. You've lost."

But Carter knew better.

"Max, Max," said the Piper. "You keep surprising me. How'd you find your way back here to the Summer Isle?"

"The Black Door, the one you locked."

The Piper chuckled, then winced at the pain in his ribs. "Of course. And being a human child who'd set foot on the Summer Isle, you had the power to unlock it. I should have thought of that."

"Yeah, you should've." Max held up her sword threateningly.

Carter put a hand on her arm. "Max, relax." They weren't here to fight him. Not if they could help it.

"Look, my sister is right, Piper. It's over."

The Piper *tsk*ed. "You know better than that, Carter."

Max nudged Carter. "What's he talking about?"

"The pipe's not really burning," said Carter. "Look at it closely, Max."

The flames blazed around the magical pipe, but the wood wasn't blackened or charred. It was perfect, untouched by the heat.

The Piper let his hand hover over the flames. "The Peddler couldn't bring himself to destroy my pipe, the sentimental old fool. So that fire won't hurt it." The Piper briefly touched the flames, then yanked his fingers back. "Can't say the same about my fingers, though." He pulled off his hood and looked directly at Carter. "I need you to get it for me, Carter."

Max laughed out loud at him. "What?"

But Carter wasn't laughing. Not this time. "You think I can get the pipe out of the fire? What if there's some other magical trap or something?"

"You opened my prison. And the magic that kept me captive there is the same magic that keeps my pipe locked away here. The Peddler's magic. It's why I wanted you with me, and now here you are. I know you can do it."

"You knocked me off a cliff."

"I lost my temper. I'm sorry about that."

"I'd like to throw *him* off a cliff," said Max.

"Even if you're right, why in the world should I help you?" asked Carter.

"Because, Carter, you've already lost the war! Look around you. Snow, eternal night. The Peddler's dead. The Summer Isle was doomed the minute I set foot on it." The Piper turned away. "I know that now."

"That can't be true!" said Max. "I brought hundreds of people back with me. They're just looking for a home."

"Then you brought them to their doom instead."

Max grabbed her brother's arm. "Carter, there has to be something we can do. There has to be a way to fix it."

But Carter didn't know what to say to her. Whatever poison Grannie had unleashed in the land with the Peddler's murder, it didn't look like it was fading. The Summer Isle truly looked lost.

"If I give you your pipe back, can you take the children

of Hamelin home again?" asked Carter. "Not just back to our world, but back to *their* time. Can they go home for real?"

"No," said the Piper. "I'm being honest with you, Carter. It can't be done."

"Then what was all this for?" cried Carter. "The prophecy said I'd lead them home again, but all I've done is make things worse. Everything I do is wrong!"

"Not everything." The Piper took a step forward. "I'd forgotten what it was like to be around other people. And you . . . reminded me of that. I taught you magic, but you taught me things, too. With my pipe, I can be sure you all get safely away from this place, and back to New Hamelin. From there, you can use the Black Door to escape to your world, take the others with you. Cut your losses and run. Escape this Winter Isle."

"If I say no, we could still walk out of here," said Carter. "We could still use the Black Door."

The Piper nodded. "You could. But it's on the other side of the isle, and Wormling's army is still out there. The rat king will soon set his sights on New Hamelin. Can you get there in time?"

Carter looked at his sister, but Max emphatically shook her head. She didn't trust the Piper, and she was right not to. Lukas had said it many times: the Piper was the reason all of this began. But was he? Grannie Yaga had revealed herself to be the real power behind everything that had gone wrong, starting with corrupting the Piper. They'd all been touched by the witch's evil.

Despite everything, Carter couldn't believe the Piper

wanted to hurt the children of Hamelin. But he'd let his desire for vengeance for his mother's death blind him to the danger he was putting them in. In many ways, he was blind still.

Carter's mind made up, he took a step toward the fire.

Max grabbed him by the arm. "Carter!"

"I know what I'm doing, Max. We have all those people to think about. Trust me, okay?"

Reluctantly, his sister let him go.

The flames danced in the wind, but they didn't go out. They burned as bright and as hot as ever. At the center, the pipe waited.

"So I just grab it, huh?" said Carter.

"Yes," said the Piper.

"And if I get burned, too?"

"You won't."

"Carter!" warned Max. "He's not on our side!"

"No, I'm not," snapped the Piper. "I don't care about sides, but I never wanted the children of Hamelin to get hurt. I'd rather see you lead them home than suffer an eternity of winter and darkness, to leave them at the mercy of Wormling's rats. I swear that much."

Carter closed his eyes; he tried to drown out their arguing. It all came down to this.

He found his focus, his center. He reached out a hand. The fire did not burn him.

The pipe was within his grasp now. Just inches away.

He heard the Piper exclaim breathlessly, "It's working!"

Carter's fingers found the pipe. It was surprising

because he'd half expected to feel something special about it. But it felt like an ordinary pipe. Nothing remarkable at all. Smooth polished wood. Almost fragile.

And in that moment, as Carter wrapped his fingers around the magic flute of the Pied Piper of Hamelin, two things became clear to him. Beyond any doubt, he knew these things to be true:

One, he could destroy this pipe.

It wasn't indestructible, far from it. This was just a simple flute, the kind a poor mother gifts to her only child. It had no power, no more significance than that. But for the Piper, it was enough. His humanity, what was left of it, was bound up in that pipe, along with the memory of a mother's love. Without it, the Piper's magic was weak indeed.

It wouldn't take much. The Piper would never again threaten the children of any world. Carter had magic enough to shatter it into a thousand pieces. He could probably break it with his bare hands.

And, two, he wasn't going to.

Up until that moment, Carter's quest had been clear to him—keep the Piper from getting his pipe, no matter what. What had changed? Carter had come to know the Piper better than anyone else had, with the exception perhaps of the Peddler. And the Piper had said it himself—the Peddler could have destroyed the pipe, but he didn't. Perhaps because he'd hoped the Piper would someday be worthy of it again.

It was up to Carter to decide if that someday was now.

Carter lifted the pipe from the flames.

The Piper's eyes widened with longing. "At last," he murmured. "Give it to me!"

"Don't do it," said Max.

Carter looked up at his sister just in time to see her recoil with horror. Then something struck her across the face as clawed fingers yanked Carter backward by the hair. The pipe slipped from his fingers and fell to the floor with a clatter.

A checkered cloak brushed past him as the Piper lunged for his fallen pipe, while a spindly creature in torn and tattered rags twisted its fingers in Carter's hair. A gray man had appeared out of nowhere, and now it had him.

Carter heard the flapping of wings, and in his periphery he could just make out a large winged shape silhouetted against the moon. Carter's heart sank as the creature flew in through the open wall and stretched itself into a sickeningly familiar shape.

"No!" cried Max.

"Now, now, Maxine, dearie," cooed Grannie. "You stay put or I'll have to do something just awful to your brother." Her flesh was charred and blistered, her hair burned clean away, but the witch was still alive. And she was smiling—jagged metal teeth in a crooked grin.

The Piper joined her side as he cradled his pipe lovingly against his chest.

Grannie Yaga clapped her hands together. "I win!"

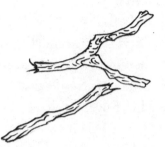

CHAPTER TWENTY-SIX

"Take a step closer with that sword, and I'll have the gray man wring your brother's neck."

Max had caught a glimpse of the gray man as he slinked out from the shadows at the base of the pillars, but too late. The creature must've been there all along, just waiting for Carter to rescue the Piper's pipe.

Grannie Yaga had appeared seconds after, swooping down from the night sky in her bird shape. Hideously burned, one eye missing—but the witch gloated because, despite it all, she'd emerged the victor. She'd outmaneuvered them.

Max's cheek stung from where the gray man had struck her. Her eyes were full of tears, and not just because of the pain. She was caught in a standoff with the witch and didn't know what to do next. Grannie's magic couldn't hurt her as long as she held the sword, but Carter was at the mercy of that monster.

"Now," said Grannie, eyeing Max warily. "I seen what Carter is capable of, and I know what that cursed sword can do, so I've told my gray friend there that if the boy so much as blinks the wrong way, he's to snap his neck. That goes for you, too, little miss. Don't anyone think of playing the hero. That time's past."

Grannie stumbled a little as she took an uneasy step forward, but the Piper reached out to steady her. "There's a good boy," she said, patting him on the cheek. "But your Grannie can manage. Believe it or not, I been in worse shape than this. Carter's not the first one to try and burn a witch!"

Max felt sick. Her knees were shaking. She was terrified that she was about to lose her brother, that she was probably about to die herself. But most of all, she was mad. Angry. Furious because the Piper had betrayed them.

Just like she'd known he would.

"You had this planned all along?" The words tasted so bitter in her mouth that she nearly spat them out. Her fingers gripped the sword's hilt so tightly that her knuckles turned white. "For a moment I believed you actually had a soul."

The Piper glanced at her, then quickly pulled his hood up and turned away.

"Aw," said Grannie. "Don't you go hurting the boy's feelings! He's sensitive. Always has been. Too much time spent with your brother got his head messed up. I explained things to him proper, you see. Brought him back around to the correct way of thinking. Told him that Carter wouldn't ever give him the pipe willingly; the boy would destroy it the first chance he got—but first he had to be tricked into rescuing it from the fire. Trust is a lie. The only friend the Piper has now, or will ever have, is me."

"That's not true!" cried Carter. "I did trust you, Piper! You didn't give me a chance!"

Grannie glared at him. "The war's over. The land of dreams is now the land of nightmares, the isle of witches! The Piper will help his Grannie rule, won't you, dear? We'll turn the Black Tower's prison into a throne room."

The witch's gaze settled on Max as Grannie smacked her cracked, blackened lips. "And in return the Piper will bring children to visit old Grannie whenever she asks. But first, we have our little standoff to settle. Put down the sword, or your brother dies."

"You're going to kill us anyway!"

"Maybe. But you want to watch him go first?"

A sob broke through Max's defenses. She didn't want to cry in front of this hateful creature. But she couldn't watch Carter die. . . .

Grannie waved her hand impatiently. "Give the sword over to the Piper, girl, and I'll make it quick."

Max glanced at the Piper, but he wasn't watching any of it. He just cradled his pipe, stroking it lovingly the way one would pet a kitten.

"Piper!" Grannie snapped.

"Hmm?"

"The Peddler's sword!"

The Piper turned to Max.

Choking back her tears, Max decided there and then that she would go down fighting. "I'm sorry, Carter," she whispered.

But the Piper didn't move. He just watched her. Then he looked at Carter and Grannie, in turn. It was almost as if he was just then noticing he wasn't alone up there. "I've been thinking about mirrors."

"What's that, boy?" barked Grannie. "Make sense."

"You gave me a mirror once, Grannie. A magic mirror."

"Yes, yes," she said impatiently. "And thanks to that mirror, you're free and you have your lovely pipe back. You're welcome. Now, do as I—"

"What did you use it for, Grannie?"

Grannie sucked on her teeth as she stared at the Piper. Max didn't understand what was going on between them, but she took advantage of the distraction to inch a step closer to her brother.

"Piper, *dear,* everything I did was for your own good."

But the Piper continued, his face deadly serious. "Someone stole the Winter Children from the elves. While I was collecting the children of Hamelin, someone else was stealing the elves' children away. Was it you?"

"I don't think I like your tone—"

His voice rising, the Piper repeated the question. "Was it you?"

Grannie visibly flinched. "Yes! I took the elves' children from them. I chased them through the mirror into the world of humankind. I needed you to see that there is only one person in two worlds who cares for you. Me!"

"You mean you wanted to hurt the Princess and it didn't matter that she blamed me." The Piper nodded slowly. "You know, I felt sorry for you once. A lonely old woman in a dingy hut. I'd visit you and play songs for you, remember?

And all the while, you whispered in my ear ... told me to trust you. Told me to steal the children of Hamelin away."

"Yes."

"Then, when I did what you asked, you turned everyone against me."

Grannie laughed in the Piper's face, a hollow cackle that drowned out the howling wind. "They were already against you, boy! Do you think the Peddler was your friend? The beautiful *Princess,* maybe? Oh, that's rich! The Peddler pitied you and the Princess feared you, because she knew what you really are. The people of your village had it right, you know? The *Son of the Witch* they named you, and who can love a little witch boy but another witch? Who's left for you now but Grannie? I'm all there is." She pointed a long finger at the Piper. "And you belong to me!"

"No, you don't," said Carter. "You don't have to listen to her, Piper!"

"Shut him up!" snarled Grannie.

Carter's words were quickly stifled as the gray man tightened his grip.

Max didn't know what to do. Another word from Grannie, and Carter was dead. She blurted out the only thing that came to mind. "She's lying! The Peddler cared!"

The Piper glanced at her. "What?"

"She's a fool girl," said Grannie. "Pay her no mind."

But Max kept barreling on. She wasn't very good at this—talking was her brother's thing—but she had to try. "The Peddler made me promise him, before he agreed to help us rescue Carter ... He made me promise that if I could save you I would. He was afraid I'd be so mad I'd want you dead, and honestly I did, but he made me promise to spare your life anyway."

The Piper stared at her, wordless.

"See?" said Max. "After all that happened, he still cared about you. He died still caring about you. And you know, you *know,* that my brother cares about you, too!"

"Enough lies!" Grannie narrowed her one good eye at Max. "Quite the speech, dear. Want to hear my rebuttal?" The witch grinned. "Kill the boy."

"No!" Max screamed, but she couldn't even hear her own voice. It was drowned out by the playing of a flute.

Time went into slow motion as the magic of the Piper's music washed over her. Max watched, without a care in the world, as the gray man let go of her brother and strolled over to the watch fire. It turned to the Piper briefly, as if to ask, "Here?" Then it stepped into the flame and disappeared in a puff of ash and smoke.

Grannie, on the other hand, had her hands clutched to her ears. She was frothing at the mouth as she tried to resist the Piper's spell, even as the Piper's fingers played furiously over his flute. The witch and the Piper were caught in a battle of wills, but Max wanted to go over and tell Grannie that it was all okay. Why didn't she just listen to the music? Why didn't she just do what the music asked? But she didn't, because the music had told Max to stay put, stay out of danger.

Carter did not seem to be enjoying the music; he seemed barely even to hear it. He was too busy doing something with his hands.

Fire exploded around Grannie even as she hurled waves of killing frost from her fingertips. The Piper nimbly dodged her attacks, while Carter fended them off with his own magic fire.

Grannie Yaga threw herself at the Piper, and the music stopped as they fell to the ground. Max came back to her senses just as Grannie sank her teeth into the Piper's wrist. The Piper cried out and his magic flute fell from his grasp. It rolled and came to a rest at the very edge of the lighthouse, where the floor met the sky.

Grannie released the Piper from her jaws and snarled at Carter and Max like a wild animal cornered.

Max raised her sword.

The Piper meanwhile, clutching his wounded arm to his chest, reached for his fallen pipe. But the ground was slick now with the Piper's own blood. He slipped.

"Max!" cried Carter, pointing to the Piper, who was dangling over the side by one hand.

Max grabbed the Piper's wrist just as he started to slide. The sea crashed against the rocks far below.

The Piper's hand was bloody, making it hard to get a good hold on him. But inch by inch, she helped the Piper crawl back to safety.

He was almost there when an explosion rocked the lighthouse. The floor shook beneath their feet. Pieces of masonry fell from the ceiling. Max dropped the sword as she struggled not to drop the Piper. She squeezed her eyes shut and put every bit of strength into not letting go. "Hold on!" she cried.

The Piper was safe, but he wasn't listening to Max. His

eyes were on her brother. "Carter!" he warned. "It's too much! You'll kill yourself!"

Her brother's face was white, teeth clenched in concentration as he tried to shield himself from Grannie's magical onslaught. Max could see him losing control. Flames flared all around him.

"Let it go, Carter!" the Piper yelled.

A second explosion rocked the lighthouse tower. They were buffeted by alternating waves of heat and cold as the Piper and Max clung together to keep from being blown off the ledge.

As the dust finally began to settle, Max spotted her brother. Carter lay with his back against a pillar. His crutch lay in pieces around him, and he wasn't moving.

Grannie stood triumphantly over him. "Powerful magic you've got, boy. A little more training, and you might've been a match for me. I can see why the prophecy chose you. But the prophecy never said nothing about you living in the end, now, did it?"

Max screamed her brother's name. His eyes fluttered open. He groaned. Max searched for the sword. In the blast it had been blown clear to the other side of the brazier, well out of her reach.

Grannie called over her shoulder. "Be with you in a minute, dear. One child at a time."

Just then, a small, furry head peeked out from behind the watch-fire brazier. "Hello, Grannie!"

The witch whipped around, fingers outstretched threateningly. When she saw Bandybulb, she cackled. "You! I've got a new cage for you—just you wait."

But Bandybulb made a dash for the Sword of the Eldest Boy.

"What do you think you're doing, little kobold?" Grannie eyed the kobold with suspicion. "You think *you* can scare me with that pigsticker? You can barely lift it!"

"Nope. I'm not a fighter." Bandybulb grabbed the sword's hilt and, with all his might, slid the blade toward the open doorway, where it disappeared in the shadows. "But he is!"

A moment later, a new figure stepped into the fight. Lukas's lips were still blue, but his eyes were bright with determination. He held the Sword of the Eldest Boy in his hands.

Grannie's gloating grin melted away.

Lukas and the witch squared off, each circling the other warily. Her magic couldn't directly hurt him, not with the sword in hand. Grannie focused instead on the fallen chunks of stone all around them. Using her power, she hurled a piece of stone at Lukas, which he barely avoided. Then she hurled another. And another.

"Max," someone whispered. She turned to see the Piper at her side. His pipe was clutched in one hand and the other bled all over the stones. His face was pale.

"See there?" he whispered. "Your brother!"

As Lukas dodged the witch's attacks, Carter was crawling toward Grannie, unseen. He winced as he dragged his wounded leg across the shattered stone.

"What's he doing?" the Piper asked.

"Trying to be a hero," answered Max.

The Piper grinned. "Then let's help him. I need to stand."

Max wrapped an arm around his middle and let him lean on her as he got to his feet.

Carter was gesticulating, trying to work one last spell through the pain.

The Piper played his pipe, one-handed this time, and summoned up a gust of wind that nearly knocked Grannie off the ledge. Nearly, but not quite.

Grannie turned on him, her face twisted with rage. "Ungrateful boy! I'll stop your song once and for all!"

Lukas tried to take advantage of the distraction, and charged her, but the witch was fast. With one hand she blocked the Piper's wind, while she sent another chunk of masonry at Lukas. It bounced off his shoulder, and the boy cried out in pain.

Whatever her brother was up to, they were out of time. "Carter! Now!"

A cherry pie appeared out of thin air and exploded in Grannie's face. The eruption of cherry filling and pie crust blinded the old witch.

Lukas saw his chance. Blade outstretched, he lunged for Grannie Yaga.

The Piper stopped his song, and the wind died. For a moment, all was still.

Grannie wiped the pie from her one good eye and stared in disbelief at the sword protruding from her chest. From somewhere deep inside the witch erupted a wail like nothing Max had ever heard. Grannie Yaga threw her head back and roared even as her already blackened and charred skin began to flake and crumble.

Her screams of rage reached a crescendo, and Grannie disappeared in a blaze of light. As quickly as it lit up, the conflagration died down again—one last spark atop the lighthouse at the edge of the world.

All that was left of the witch of the Bonewood was ash.

❧ CHAPTER TWENTY-SEVEN ❧

Thy found Leetha curled up in a corner at the bottom of the lighthouse stairs. A touch of color had come back to her cheeks, and her eyes fluttered open weakly. "Did we win?" she murmured.

Carter, who himself was standing only with Max's support, gave her a tired smile. "Look." He pointed to the eastern sky. The clouds were breaking, revealing a sliver of pink. "Dawn."

Leetha peered out the doorway at the sky. "I'm sorry I missed it."

"I wouldn't have made it this far without you," said Carter.

"You know, I think I feel spring in the air!" exclaimed Bandybulb. "Or am I just overheated from all my heroics?"

Maybe the kobold was right. The sun was finally beginning to rise, and it did feel to Carter like the air was just a touch warmer than it had been on previous mornings. In any case, morning had come after all.

Carter's crutch was in pieces, so his sister helped him along the bridge, step by careful step. Lukas's strength was rapidly returning, enough so that he could assist Leetha. All the while, Bandybulb chatted cheerily about how this would be a tale to rival those of King Tussleroot.

And the Piper brought up the rear, his pipe clutched tightly in his hands and his hood pulled low over his face. He hadn't said much since Grannie's defeat, and Lukas and Leetha eyed him warily, but Carter felt differently. In that last moment, the Piper had made a choice against Grannie Yaga. He'd stood with them, and that meant something. It didn't erase his past sins, but maybe it was a start.

Carter hoped so. In any case, the Piper stayed with them, at least for the time being.

As they dragged themselves across the bridge from Magician's Landing, the pink sliver in the sky turned to sunrise. Nighttime gave over to a gray, but welcome, morning. Carter wasn't looking forward to climbing the steps back up the bluffs, but he was anxious to leave Magician's Landing behind them. They all were. When they got to the beach, they found that Grannie's hut had collapsed, and already the incoming tide was carrying pieces of it out to sea. "Good riddance," said Max.

"I dunno," said Carter. "I never got a chance to drive it."

"Neither did we," said Lukas, laughing. "All we did was get ourselves banged up inside an oven. Leave it to your sister. . . ."

The boy's words died off as he glanced up at the tall

bluffs overlooking the thin strip of beach. "Oh, no," he breathed.

As the morning sun broke over the bluffs, a shape appeared on the steps. It was a rat scout. Nose in the air, the creature sniffed and then let out a shrieking squeal that hurt Carter's teeth.

It was answered by a chorus of thousands. High above them, a horde of rats appeared atop the bluffs. They lined the cliffs as far as the eye could see, waving their wicked clubs and knives as they snarled and spat their taunts. They gnashed their teeth and shouted promises of terrible things to come. Carter and his friends were trapped, with the sea at their backs and nowhere to run.

Wormling's army had arrived.

The rat king descended the steps, surrounded by his guards. "Bow before King Wormling, you slime!" one of them shouted as they approached.

No. It was too much: to have come all this way, to have endured so much, just to see it end like this. If Carter had had the strength, he would have set the whole army on fire. He would have brought down the mountains and buried the rats beneath the rock and rubble. But he was tired. He'd nearly burned himself out in the fight with Grannie. In the last few moments of that battle, he'd known that if he'd tried to match her power spell for spell, he would have shattered like one of the Piper's pipes. Luckily, he'd had enough strength left for one simple little spell.

But conjuring pies wouldn't save them now. And when he reached for the magic, it seemed so far away—a hazy mirage on the horizon. There was nothing left to give.

And yet, he felt his sister tensing beside him. Out of the corner of his eye, Carter saw Lukas raise his sword. The boy's arms were shaking so hard, he could barely hold it. Even little Bandybulb stood his ground, tiny fists in the air.

"Kneel!" the rat snapped again.

"No," said Carter. "No."

Wormling let out a raspy laugh. "They have backbone! Children always do at first. Stubborn, slow to accept defeat even when they've already lost. But they break easy enough."

"Grannie Yaga is dead," said Max.

"The witch is dead?" said Wormling. "Best news I've heard in ages! Without her around, the ogres will probably just wander back to the Bonewood, but that's fine by me. They have a nasty habit of stepping on rats, anyway. And if I never see another gray man again, it'll be too soon."

Max took a step forward. "We did your dirty work for you. Now let us pass."

"I don't think so," answered the rat king. "Grannie's gone; the Peddler's dead. That leaves King Wormling and his rat horde to rule the Summer Isle! There's plenty to plunder, plenty to throw into chains. Starting with you children." He motioned to his guards, knives and whips at the ready.

"There's too many," whispered Max. "There's so many!"

"I won't be a slave!" called Lukas. "I'll die first."

"Your choice," said Wormling. He turned to face his army, the horde of rats thousands strong—their sleek bodies falling over one another in anticipation.

A squeal went up from the horde that made Carter want to cover his ears and hide.

"Kill them!" cried the rat king. "Kill them all!"

Like a lake spilling over a dam, the horde of rats began swarming down the great stone steps toward Carter and his friends. He tried once more to reach for the magic: he focused; he closed his eyes. . . .

And was nearly blinded by the conflagration of power before him. All the threads of magic, endless possibilities were being drawn to one spot, bound into a sweet, simple song.

He opened his eyes. The Piper was playing his pipe. Playing despite the pain of his wounded arm. The rats halted their charge. They seemed frozen by the music.

The Piper finished his tune and pulled back his hood. He breathed deep as he let the sea breeze blow across his face. "It's an old song. One of my first. The Peddler was fond . . ." He trailed off as he stared at his pipe, admiring it in the morning sunlight. It balanced perfectly in his fingers. His voice was quiet, barely loud enough for Carter to hear above the sound of the waves. "I . . . I don't know how to make amends. I don't think I've ever said I was sorry. To anyone. But I am, Carter. I'm sorry."

One by one, the rats were coming to their senses, their dazed expressions replaced with fury. They began to snarl and hiss again.

The Piper clasped Carter's shoulder. "When I was very little I used to play pretend. Back then *I* played the hero. Can you imagine that? Me?"

"Yeah, actually I can."

The Piper drew back his cloak and produced a shoulder pack he'd hidden away. As he unslung it, he said, "This is yours."

It was Carter's pack. But he had little time to wonder why the Piper still carried it, because at that moment the Piper drew a deep breath and lifted his pipe to his lips. "There's only one way to do this right. Goodbye, Carter."

Carter felt a stab of panic. "What? Wait!"

But the Piper was already playing. He walked calmly into the surging horde as he played a new song. The music, as always, was flawless. A perfect composition of notes, a soaring march. But this time there was something else beneath it. Nothing magical, at least not the kind of magic that would charm human ears, but a wealth of feeling, overflowing with bittersweet happiness, heartbreaking regret and, at last, a longing for peace.

Tears ran down Carter's cheeks as his heart broke for the beauty of the Piper's last song.

The Piper began to dance in a circle, and back toward Magician's Landing, skipping away from Carter and his friends toward the great stone bridge.

The rats followed. Wormling's guards dropped their weapons, their expressions went slack and they scurried forward on all fours. Even the rat king himself awkwardly shambled along beside them, his kingly majesty forgotten. Hundreds began spilling down the stairway, pushing and shoving and snapping to get ahead of each other.

The Piper led them farther and farther onto the ancient bridge. Soon it was packed with rats, and the Piper's song swelled, growing louder even as the rats' squeals of delight tried to drown it out.

From high up on the bluffs, the rats who couldn't make it to the steps fast enough began throwing themselves into the sea, desperate to follow the music. As Carter and his friends huddled on the beach, still more spilled past them and surged onto the bridge. They were fighting, clawing at each other to stay on, but they tumbled off the sides into the crashing waves below. Too many. Cracks appeared all along the sides. The weight was more than the timeworn structure could bear.

The bridge crumbled. The Piper's song was nearly drowned out by the roar of stone grinding against stone.

"Oh, no," breathed Carter. He felt Max's arms hold him tight, but he didn't look away.

The sea boiled white with froth as it swallowed stone and rat alike.

The song played up until the last stone fell, until Carter caught a glimpse of a checkered cloak falling into the tossing waves.

The music ended. The rat king's army was no more. The bridge was gone.

And so was the Piper.

CHAPTER TWENTY-EIGHT

Bandybulb had been right: spring was in the air. But it came gradually, a slow thaw that lasted weeks rather than hours. New buds appeared on trees as creeks overflowed with snowmelt. A proper changing of the seasons had come to the Summer Isle for the first time in memory. What had once been an isle of everlasting summer, and for a brief time everlasting winter, was now just an isle. The spell that had been broken with the Peddler's death stayed broken, but the land was no longer polluted with Grannie Yaga's dark magic, either. A new force—nature— had taken hold.

And so morning turned to afternoon turned to evening turned to night. And every day the cycle started over again. Time had come to the isle at long last.

Carter and his friends followed the coast, just in case there were any lingering ogres about. They took it slow, made camp, tended to their wounds and rested often. They kept watch at night, but no threats appeared. However, rumors followed them wherever they went. Wandering bands of kobolds spoke of a great thawing, extending even to the notorious Chillwood, home to the witch Roga. Flowers bloomed there, and the sun drove long-standing shadows away.

One early morning, Bandybulb claimed to have seen a great black ship in the sea fog. Standing at the prow, he said, was a wizened old man and a fellow in a checkered cloak. But by the time Carter had limped over, the ship—if there was one—had disappeared again into the mist.

They headed inland, turned north at the Eastern Fork and then west, steering well clear of the Bonewood. By the time they emerged from the Shimmering Forest and came within sight of New Hamelin, the days were so warm that they were forced to carry their cloaks rather than wear them.

New Hamelin had been busy. With the help of the refugees from Bordertown, they'd built an entirely new section of village, complete with extra-extra-large homes for the trollsons. The meager vegetable gardens and pigpens wouldn't be enough to feed so many hungry stomachs, so the trollsons were put to work plowing the neighboring fields so that proper crops could be planted.

Emilie and Harold met them at the gate, along with Marc and several of the other rescued children. Their collars were gone, and they'd put a little weight back on their bones. Very little was said that first day back, but many tears were shed. This time, though, they were tears of joy.

Of everyone, only Carter didn't feel like celebrating. While the others feasted and the trollsons sang bawdy songs in their deep bass voices, he sat in a cottage alone. Every now and then he'd conjure a little ball of fire and then let it wink out. The Summer Isle had changed, but there was still plenty of magic if you knew where to look. After a few hours, he got hungry and conjured a pie: apple walnut this time, as he'd turned off of cherry. He ate a full half of it and gave himself a stomachache.

There was a knock on the door in the late afternoon. Carter worried that it was Mrs. Amsel, with yet another plate of cheese and sausages. The little elfling housekeeper had been aghast at how thin everyone had gotten on their travels, especially Carter, and was on a personal mission to return them to a "healthy plumpness."

Carter had just eaten half a pie, for goodness' sake. What more could the woman want?

But it wasn't Mrs. Amsel. It was his sister.

"Hey."

"Thought you were Mrs. Amsel. Whew."

Max's eyes went wide as she spotted the half-eaten pie. "The woman's on a tear. She make you eat that all by yourself?"

"Uh . . ." Carter wiped his sticky face. "No. That was just kind of bad judgment on my part. You want some?"

Max took a seat. "You didn't conjure up silverware, did you?"

"No, but my knife's on the table. Go ahead and cut yourself a piece."

Max dug in. "Wow, so that's what a magic pie tastes like, huh? Not bad at all."

"Yeah? Wait until it explodes."

Max stopped midbite.

"Joking. That was a joke."

His sister nodded, but nevertheless she set her slice down and gently scooted it to the other side of the table. "Everyone's asking about you."

Carter shrugged. "I don't really feel like partying."

Max leaned her elbows on her knees. "How's your leg?"

He pulled the cuff of his pants up over his ankle. The sprain—and he'd been lucky it had turned out to only be a sprain—had healed, but something more unexpected had taken its place. He turned his leg so that Max could get a good look.

Carter's foot had turned in on itself. The toes curled and shriveled. The clubfoot he'd lived with almost his whole life was back.

She let out a gasp.

Carter shrugged. "Leetha says she thinks it's connected to all the changes happening on the isle, the seasons changing and everything getting older. The Peddler and Grannie were the last of the immortals, and when they died, part of the isle's magic died with them. Did you know that one of Leetha's people found a gray hair the other day? Man, I would've liked to see that temper tantrum! And I hear Finn's the first New Hameliner in seven hundred years to get a cold! Poor kid."

"Oh, Carter," said Max. "I'm so sorry."

"Don't be. The Piper kind of warned me about this, only he thought it might happen when I got home. The spell's broken. Magic that's done can be undone, he said."

Carter pulled his pants leg back down and gently set his foot back onto the floor. From behind his chair he produced a battered old shoulder pack. His pack, the one the Piper had given back to him before sacrificing himself to save them all.

He wondered if the Piper had known what would happen to the Summer Isle's magic. He must have suspected, at least. It couldn't have been easy, holding on to that pack with everything the Piper went through to get to Magician's Landing.

Carter opened the pack and pulled out a well-worn plastic-and-metal leg brace. Slowly, methodically, Carter put on the brace. Years of practice meant he didn't even have to look. His fingers knew every strap, every buckle.

The Piper's parting gift.

Max watched him, tears in her eyes. "He carried it for you?"

Carter nodded.

"But do you need it? Can you ... I mean, with your magic, can you fix yourself?"

Carter stretched out his braced leg and stood. He put weight on his bad leg, but it held. It always held.

"The Piper warned me against trying to use healing magic on myself. Leetha warned me, too. If the Summer Isle can't heal my leg anymore, then I don't think I'd better try."

Max wiped her eyes. "You know what? Sometimes I am so stupid, I could kick myself. You do *not* need to fix yourself, because you are *not* broken! You're the toughest kid I've ever met."

They were quiet for a minute.

"I sound like a greeting card, don't I?" asked Max.

"Little bit." He sat back down next to her. "I never admitted this, but when Lukas first told us about the prophecy and he said it was about *me* . . . that was the best day of my life."

"Carter . . ."

"Seriously. You know, I was suddenly special, and not in that way everyone used back home. Not because of my bad leg or anything like that. I was *chosen.* I'd never felt like that before. And then, learning magic with the Piper—I kept telling myself that I was doing it for you, and to help the children of New Hamelin, that I was being selfless. . . ." Carter punched his leg in frustration. "I wasn't! I was being selfish because I liked how it made me feel. It wasn't until I saw what the Piper did, how he sacrificed himself . . . *That's* selflessness."

Max tried to put her arm around him, but he shrugged it off. The more he talked, the more unfair it all seemed. He felt himself spiraling, getting angrier and angrier, but he couldn't help it.

"Why'd he do it, Max?" Carter asked. "There had to be another way!"

"Maybe it all happened for a reason."

"What reason? All this *magic* I can do—what's it good for? Honestly, I don't even know why I got it in the first place!"

Max took Carter's face in her hands. "I do."

In the corner of the little cottage was a trunk lined with

the softest cotton. Max opened the trunk lid and gently removed two glass jars and set them on the table. She angled
them so that Carter could get a good look at the faces of his
parents floating inside.

"This is why, Carter."

"Max, I can't—"

"It's time. We can't stay here forever."

"But what if I mess it up? Setting fires and blowing up
pies is easy; this is major stuff!"

"You won't mess it up."

"How do you know?"

"I believe in you, Carter," said Max. "And if you want
another reason, try this: you're all we've got."

"Maybe Leetha can do it."

"Leetha suggested you. She said your connection to
Mom and Dad make you the perfect person to try. The
curse was laid by a magician, and it's going to take a magician to break it. You're it, Carter. You're the only one. Mom
and Dad need you."

Max didn't know what she was asking. Conjuring pies
was one thing, but those jars contained his parents' *souls*.
He'd gotten better at magic, yes, but even in the fight with
Grannie Yaga he'd been relying mostly on instinct—he'd
just thrown everything he had at her. Carter closed his eyes.
He could see the curse as a tangle of threads around those
jars. It had taken very powerful magic to warp probability
enough to separate people from their souls, especially back
home, where magic was so rare. Carter couldn't just cut the
knots tying those jars up; he had to carefully untangle them.
One slip, and who knew what might happen?

But if Carter did nothing, what then? Max said that their bodies were still alive in a hospital somewhere, but how long could the body live without the soul?

"Okay," he said after a moment. "I'll try."

Max nodded.

"It might take a while, so why don't you wait outside and make sure no one comes in. I need to focus."

His sister gave him a kiss on the head. "You can do it," she whispered, then stepped outside and closed the door gently behind her.

Carter wiped his sweaty palms on his pants and closed his eyes. With his parents clearly in mind, focus came easily—the Piper would have been proud—but the knot of magic around both jars looked more intimidating than ever. He tested the knot, a light tug here, a push there. He was prodding, looking for any weakness that might untie the tangled possibilities. After ten minutes or so of testing, he sighed.

Time to just choose a string and get to work.

✦

The moon was high in the sky when Carter heard a light knock on the door. "Yeah," he called.

Max creaked open the door. The burning brand in her hand cast the room in torchlight. Carter hadn't even realized he'd been sitting in the dark.

"You okay?" she asked. Her face was a mask of worry.

Carter's fingertips were raw, as if he'd been tugging on actual ropes instead of invisible strings. His mouth was dry and lips were chapped, and he felt as if he hadn't slept in days. He sat staring at the two open jars on the table.

When Max saw them her hand went to her mouth. "Are they . . . ? Did they . . . ?"

He looked up blankly at his sister. "They're free. Their spirits returned to their bodies back home, but before they left, Dad winked at me. He never winks."

Then Carter smiled. "Max, they're waiting for us!"

And Max was so happy, she shouted something very inappropriate. But just this once, Carter wouldn't tell Mom and Dad.

ᏯCHAPTER TWENTY-NINEᏰ

Max and Carter were awake into the small hours of the night making plans—what they'd do when they got back to New York. (Carter was dying for ice cream, of all things.) In the morning, Lukas and Emilie appeared at their door with breakfast. Over fresh-baked pumpkin bread and hard cheese, Max and Carter shared the news about their parents. Lukas and Emilie were genuinely happy, but after all the hugs and congratulations came other news.

"We're not coming with you," said Lukas.

On some level Max had been expecting this. Carter looked like he'd been doused with a bucket of cold water.

"Wh-what?" sputtered her brother. "Why? We can find a place—"

Emilie shook her head. "Your world isn't our world. Not anymore."

"But maybe that's not so bad. There's video games . . . air-conditioning. You guys are gonna love air-conditioning."

Max put her hand on her brother's shoulder. "Carter. Over a hundred orphans from the year 1284. Think about it."

He shrugged it off. "But I was supposed to lead you home! What about that stupid prophecy?"

Lukas sat down next to Carter. "Maybe you have. I think most of us said goodbye to our old lives long ago. We accepted it. What was harder was accepting that the Summer Isle could ever be any kind of home."

"The seasons pass," said Emilie. "Things here are growing, changing. Can I tell them what else, Lukas?"

At once Lukas's face turned bright red and he looked away. "Aw, Emilie. If you must."

The Eldest Girl grinned. "And Lukas has started to shave."

"What?" cried Max. Then she noticed Lukas's face deepen to a near purple. "Sorry. I just mean, wow."

"Time now passes in the Summer Isle." Emilie smoothed her shawl. "It's passing for us, too. After seven centuries of childhood, we're finally growing up. The rats are gone. The Bordertowners you brought with you, the elflings and trollsons and all the rest, they are intent on building a home here. So will we. We can finally live our lives, Carter. Thanks to you."

"Leetha's become very protective of the refugees," added Lukas. "Some of those Bordertowners out there are descendants of the original Winter Children, and some of them have children of their own. She's pledged to open the borders of the Deep Forest. She says it's past time that children played in the trees there again. You should see her when she talks about them. It's the first time she's smiled where I don't get the feeling she's picturing me hanging by my toes."

"Carter's right, you know," said Max. "Air-conditioning's pretty great. You're missing out."

With absolute earnestness Lukas said, "Maybe you can bring us some when you come to visit?"

Max could barely stifle her laugh. "You can't carry air-conditioning . . . Oh, never mind."

❖

A small group assembled to finally see them off: Lukas and Emilie, Harold, Leetha and Bandybulb. Mrs. Amsel stood beside Max and Carter, with her bag packed to overflowing with food. Never mind that the trip through the portal would last all of a few seconds; once they stepped through the Black Door, they would still have to find their way out of the Bordertown caves and back to the city surface. Mrs. Amsel wanted to make sure they could stop for snacks.

The little elfling woman had tied her kerchief up again to hide her ears. Max had been a little surprised when the former housekeeper had announced that she would be returning with them, back to a world where she would have to hide. But when pressed, Mrs. Amsel nodded and said, "Yes, it's a world of fearful people and ignorant people and those who'd never understand a little woman with pointed ears—but it's my world, too. It belongs to me as much as to them."

In truth, Max was happy to have the woman along. She was one person they wouldn't have to say goodbye to.

Bandybulb blubbered into his silk handkerchief and cried all over his fancy new waistcoat. King Tussleroot had been so delighted to see Bandybulb still alive that he'd knighted Bandybulb on the spot, declaring him Sir Bandybulb, Big Muckety-Muck and Know-It-All (a title with an impressive heritage, Tussleroot claimed). Never mind that this meant that Tussleroot's kingdom now consisted of exactly one king and a knight—in Tussleroot's opinion that only made the kingdom more impressive.

Leetha didn't cry, of course. Though she still looked like the elf girl Max had always known, there was also a new regal quality about her, or perhaps it had been there all along. "The Summer Isle owes you two a great debt, you know," she said.

Carter shook his head. "We started all this."

"No," Leetha said firmly. "Grannie Yaga was going to make her move eventually. The witch was craftier than any of us gave her credit for, but in the end she was beaten." The elf girl, the Princess, placed one palm on Carter's cheek, the other on Max's. "My heroes."

Some hero. Max's stomach was so filled with butterflies, she felt like she was going to throw up. But maybe they hadn't done *too* badly.

"Harold," Max said, "thanks for everything."

The trollson offered her his good-natured smile. "It's been fun! And the Bordertowners owe you for giving them a new home." He took a deep breath. "I think we're going to like it here."

Harold gave Max a bear hug, squeezing the air out of her in the process.

"Sorry," he added.

"No problem," said Max, gasping for breath.

When she turned around, Lukas and Emilie were giving something to Carter: a sheaf of parchment that Max recognized immediately. "Guys, you can't!"

"Aw, c'mon, Max," begged Carter. "It's cool!"

The Peddler's map had once again rearranged itself to show the Summer Isle, only now a bright dot glowed just beyond the little spot labeled *New Hamelin*. It was the exact spot they were standing in, just outside the Black Door. Max was sure it hadn't been there before.

"The Way Home," Max read.

"The map shows the path you must take, isn't that right?" said Emilie. "This is yours now. And maybe, someday, it'll show you the Summer Isle again. We can only hope."

More hugs were exchanged until at last the only person left to say goodbye to was Lukas. He was having trouble looking Max in the eye.

"No sword?" she said.

Lukas glanced down at his empty belt and smiled. "Marc is Eldest Boy again. I can just be . . . Lukas, for a change."

"Congratulations," said Max. "But I was kind of hoping you'd give the sword to me as a going-away present."

Lukas laughed. "What'll you do when you get home?"

"Besides find our mom and dad? I think I'll re-dye my hair. Roots are showing."

Lukas gave Max a hug. It was awkward at first, but eventually they gave over to it and just held each other for a few moments. It was enough to soften the hurt of leaving.

"All right," said Carter. "I guess this is it."

Max joined her brother and Mrs. Amsel at the door. The others stood in a line, waving.

"Before we go," said Max to her brother, "I have to ask, this whole magic thing—I mean, will you still be doing spells and stuff when we get home?"

"I really don't know," said Carter. "Maybe. Maybe not. You said that there are still magical beings left on earth, right? And there was at least one magician?"

"Yeah, but Vodnik was about as nasty a magician as could be. Plus, he's dead."

Carter rubbed his hands together. "Then maybe it's time someone better stepped up to the plate."

"Carter the magician?"

Her brother grinned. "Let's see."

Max put one arm around her brother. She wrapped her other arm around Mrs. Amsel, and the three of them stepped up to the door together.

"Yeah," said Max. "Let's see!"

And in a flash of magic, they were gone.

❧ EPILOGUE ❧

Summer

I f Carter didn't stop fidgeting, Max was going to have to physically restrain him. He got up from the bench, looked around, peered down the concrete path, looked again in both directions, sat down. And repeated.

"What time did you tell her?" he asked. Again.

"One o'clock," answered Max.

"And what time is it now?"

"Still not one o'clock, so will you just relax?"

Carter plopped back down on the bench beside her with an impatient sigh.

"Read your book," suggested Max.

Her brother took her advice and opened a dog-eared copy of *Prince Caspian* by C. S. Lewis. Every now and then he'd shake his head and mutter, "They're doing it all wrong," or "That was too easy!"

Critiquing the magical adventures of others had become a favorite pastime of Carter's over the last year, and soon he'd start lecturing Max on the benefits of using a painting versus a wardrobe as your magic portal—why not just an ordinary door? Max didn't know and she didn't care.

Maybe she should've just let him fidget.

"Oh, c'mon," said Carter, waving the book in the air. "They each get a magic treasure? We did it all with one sword and a map!"

"Oh my God, it's just a book, Carter!" Max snapped, and immediately regretted it. "Sorry. I guess I'm a little nervous, too."

"It's okay. I figured, you wearing a dress and all. Gotta be *super* nervous."

"What? It's a sundress and it's, like, ninety degrees outside. This is sensible, okay?"

Carter shrugged. "You say so."

Besides, she still had on her Doc Martens.

As her brother went back to reading and quietly mumbling to himself, Max surreptitiously checked her phone. No new texts, and it was officially after one o'clock. Not that Mrs. Amsel would actually know how to text. The little elfling woman distrusted smartphones.

Mrs. Amsel had turned out to be an exceptionally frugal housekeeper, and though she'd saved up a nice nest egg for her retirement, a nice nest egg went a lot further in Hamelin, Germany, than it did in New York City. One of the first things Max and Carter made Mrs. Amsel do upon arriving was buy a scratch-off lottery ticket. . . .

Now she lived in a plush apartment on Manhattan's wealthy Upper East Side. But old habits died hard, and she still tried to tidy up whenever she came over to the Webers' apartment for a visit.

She was never late, and Max had specifically chosen the Ramble because it was Mrs. Amsel's favorite part of Central Park. The little German housekeeper, who loved learning new American idioms, liked to say she knew the trails like the back of her hand. She should've been here by now.

Max caught a whiff of cigarette smoke and glared in the direction of two young guys playing a game of chicken on a fallen tree in the nearby creek, despite the signs clearly asking visitors to stay on the path. Now one of them had lit a cigarette.

"Just ignore them," said Carter, sensing Max's ire.

"Kills me when idiots like that take the park for granted. Bad enough they're polluting the air with their stupid cigarette smoke—"

"*Hallo!*"

Max looked up to see Mrs. Amsel trudging up the opposite path. The ruddy-cheeked old woman was huffing and puffing in the hot sun, but smiling. Behind her walked two tall teens. As Mrs. Amsel had told Max's parents, she had her niece and nephew visiting from Germany. They were shy, didn't know much English and were very, very provincial.

Lukas was tugging self-consciously at his starched white shirt, and Emilie had on a garish yellow-and-green blouse—a blouse! Both wore khaki shorts with white socks that ended just below their knees.

"We are getting them away from Mrs. Amsel and taking them shopping first thing," whispered Max. "They are a fashion emergency."

"Yeah."

Lukas and Emilie couldn't stop staring up at the city skyline above the trees. That is, until they spotted Max and Carter. Emilie squealed and ran forward, grabbing up both of them in a big hug. The girl was gushing, but Max couldn't understand a word she was saying.

"Slow down," said Max, laughing.

Emilie cocked her head at her and laughed herself. "Good to see you!" she said, in halting English.

"Oh, of course," said Carter. "We're outside the Summer Isle, so the Babel-fish spell doesn't work."

"Huh?" asked Max.

"She's speaking old German," explained Carter. "Her native language."

Emilie shrugged and held up her fingers just an inch apart. "Little English."

"It's okay," said Carter. "We'll just have to start working on our German, too."

Max wasn't sure if the girl understood everything Carter had just said, but she smiled and nodded anyway. Lukas hung back, looking less sure of himself.

He'd grown taller in the year they'd been apart, and much of the boy in his face was gone. The lanky arms had filled out with long, lean muscle. Max was suddenly self-conscious and found herself fixing her hair.

Lukas frowned and pointed at it.

"What?" asked Max. "Something in my hair?"

Lukas shook his head and said something Max didn't understand. He took a breath and struggled to find the words. "Good," he said, and gave her an awkward thumbs-up.

He liked her hair? "Oh, you mean the color?"

He nodded and smiled as he reached out and pointed to the pink stripe down the side. Max had let her natural color come back in except for that single stripe.

As his fingers brushed against her scalp, she felt her cheeks burning.

"Well," said Carter. "Your hair may not be quite as pink, but your cheeks sure are. Blush much, Juliet?"

Max elbowed him in the arm. Hard.

"I am teaching them English," said Mrs. Amsel. "And they are fast learners, but spending time with you two will be good for them. I'll have them speaking English like an old woman!"

"How long can you stay?" asked Carter.

Emilie seemed to get the gist of his question and conferred with Lukas. "Summer," she said after a moment. "Then back for harvest."

Two months. Two months *this* visit, Max had to remind herself. There was no reason why they couldn't come and go through the Black Door, as long as they were careful to keep it a secret. They'd already started to conspire with Mrs. Amsel to take a trip with her to "Germany" the next year. It would be good to see Harold again. Max wondered how tall the trollson had gotten.

While she hated keeping secrets from her mom and

dad, they all agreed it was for the best. Her parents had awoken from their strange comas with no memory of what had happened to them. After a battery of medical tests failed to find anything wrong with them, they returned home. If nothing else, the strange and frightening experience had forced the two of them to slow down and spend time together, and to stop taking each other for granted. Their father was still working on completing his book on the legend of the Pied Piper of Hamelin, but now he put away his papers at night when their mother got home, and weekends were reserved for the family. (That part was both a blessing and a curse.)

Overall, things were good between them again, better than they'd been in a long time, and neither Max nor Carter wanted to risk upsetting them with the unbelievable truth about the Summer Isle and all their children had been through. As Mrs. Amsel might say, better to let sleeping dogs lie.

Still, what would their parents make of Mrs. Amsel's "niece and nephew," who acted like they'd never seen a skyscraper before, because they hadn't?

Lukas put a hand on Carter's shoulder and slowly said, "You were right, Carter. Air-conditioning is ... magic!" Again he gave a thumbs-up, and they all laughed.

But someone else was laughing, too. They'd gotten the attention of the two young men smoking. One was speaking in a ridiculously faux foreign language and the other was pointing to Lukas's and Emilie's socks (which admittedly were pretty terrible). The water in the creek beneath them was littered with cigarette butts.

"Hey, go back to France," one of them called.

France? Morons.

Lukas might not have understood what they were saying, but he understood their intent. He took a protective step forward, his hands balling into fists at his side.

"Ooh, what are you going to do?" one of them called. "Come on over here, and you'll get your butt kicked."

No doubt Lukas would make quick work of these two wannabe tough guys, but the last thing they needed was to start a fistfight. Max took Lukas gently by the arm and shook her head. "They're not worth it."

Carter came around to Lukas's other side. "Yeah, I'll teach you the English word for *jerks.* Which is, well, *jerks.*"

"Look at that," called one of them. "He needs a girl and a cripple to stand up for him!"

Max whirled around. "What did you just say?"

"Max," warned Carter, but those two had gone too far.

The jerk with the cigarette smirked at her. "I called your little buddy there a cripple, and you a girl. But I know a better word for what you are. . . ."

That was it. Max had stood up to far worse than a couple of bullies. Those two didn't know what they were getting themselves into.

But Carter blocked her way. "No," he said firmly. "Let's just ignore them and leave."

"Carter, you heard what he said!"

"Yeah, and it was just a word. A stupid word that only a couple of jerks would use, anyway. But it's not worth getting into a fight, okay?"

Max took a deep breath. The two guys were chuckling

to themselves and whispering. Lukas stood next to her, glowering. All he needed was permission.

"You're right," said Max. "Let's just go."

"Such boys," said Mrs. Amsel, shaking her head. "No manners."

Max took Emilie's arm in hers. "Let's get out of here and introduce you two to some of the good things about this city. Let's start with pizza."

"Air-conditioning?" suggested Lukas.

As Max and her friends gathered their things, the two boys continued to laugh and taunt them with insults, but they made no move to follow.

"Everyone ready?" asked Max. "Carter?"

Her brother had his book open again. He held it in front of his face like he was reading, but Max could see that his eyes were closed.

"You okay?" she whispered.

"Fine," he whispered back. "Just focusing."

A sudden *crack* split the air as the fallen tree the two bullies were standing on snapped right down the middle. Both boys were thrown off balance and fell, screaming, headfirst into the filthy creek water below.

"Help, I can't swim!" one of them called.

"Just stand up, you idiot!" said his friend as he realized the creek was only hip-deep.

Still, the two of them were drenched and covered head to toe in muck. One of them had a cigarette butt plastered to his wet head.

As they left the park, it was Max's turn to laugh. Lukas, Emilie and even Mrs. Amsel joined in.

As their laughter died down, Mrs. Amsel wiped her eyes. "My goodness! What were the odds that the tree would break at precisely the right moment?"

Max smiled knowingly at her brother. "What do you say?"

"I don't know," Carter answered. "One in a million, maybe?"

THANK YOU

The road back from the Summer Isle has been a long one, and many people helped guide this book along the way. Thanks to Craig Phillips for the beautiful covers. Thanks to Team Hamelin—Stephen Brown and Kelly Delaney— for their valuable notes throughout the series. Thanks to Michele Burke for taking a chance on this story in the first place, and especially to Michelle Frey, who put so much hard work into these books and constantly amazed me with her energy and insight (she has to be so sick of rats by now, my goodness!). As always, thanks to my agent and friend, Kate Schafer Testerman (who, come to think of it, must also be sick of rats). And last, my love and gratitude go to Alisha and Willem for putting up with this cranky guy typing away at his desk.

ABOUT MATTHEW

Matthew Cody is the author of *The Peddler's Road* and *The Magician's Key*, the first two books in the Secrets of the Pied Piper trilogy, as well as the popular Supers of Noble's Green trilogy: *Powerless, Super,* and *Villainous.* He is also the author of *Will in Scarlet* and *The Dead Gentleman.* Originally from the Midwest, he now lives with his wife and son in Manhattan. You can visit him on the Web at matthewcody.com.